And
MARVEL

Tales for Well-Dressed Cynics
and Optimistic Ragamuffins

And
MARVEL

Cathleen Davies

4 Horsemen
Publications, Inc.

4 Horsemen
Publications, Inc.

4 Horsemen Publications, Inc.
1497 Main St. Suite 169
Dunedin, FL 34698
4horsemenpublications.com
info@4horsemenpublications.com

Cover & Typesetting by Autumn Skye
Edited by Jen Paquette

Library of Congress Control Number: 2022948704

Paperback ISBN-13: 979-8-8232-0139-1
Hardcover ISBN-13: 978-1-64450-727-8
Audiobook ISBN-13: 979-8-8232-0137-7
Ebook ISBN-13: 979-8-8232-0138-4

Dedication

To DC, obviously

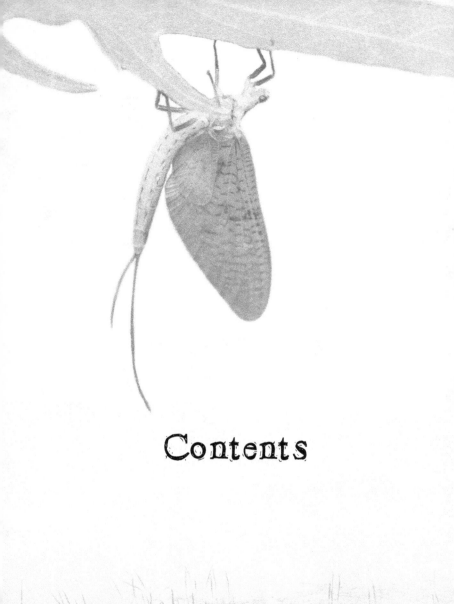

Contents

Acknowledgements

I need to show some gratitude before anyone starts reading. In this book, there's a small chance I've portrayed people unflatteringly. This is wrong. Here are some corrections and thankyous that I think are important to make in my new, presumably temporary, state of stability.

To The Girl: You deserve to be named, but I know that's not possible. I know I've thanked you quite intensely already, but it bears repeating. Thank you. You've been more significant to me than you know.

To good, kind, American friend: Cheers for all the tea, mate.

To Mutual Friend of Great Importance: I have been unfair to you, but only because your opinion mattered so much to me. Your support kept me together, and your wisdom is indisputable. I'm sorry I entangled you unhealthily in my recovery. It must have been difficult. That comment about DC not liking my work has been let go because I know how much you loved him too. I care about you deeply. Thank you for being there.

To G4 in general: The whole lot of you are good, good people.

To Deej specifically: You helped me feel less alone by telling your story. I hope people might feel less alone reading mine.

To all my friends in el País Vasco: Thank you for putting up with me when I was so unwell, for helping me with Spanish, and for buying all those cañas. I hope we meet again when things are slightly better.

To my parents: Thanks for raising me. Sorry all your kids turned out to be difficult or mentally ill. I know I was supposed to be the easy one.

To DC's mother ("Mother"): I can't imagine your pain. I can only view it as an intensified version of my own. During the funeral, you cried and held my hands and told me that your boy "had good taste." You don't know how much this meant to me. Thank you for all the gifts from his will. Thank you for forgiving me. I'm sorry I was cruel and defensive at times, both in speaking to you, and in the way I've written this. I know I could have handled things better. I was in pain, but it was still wrong. I will always send you well-wishes and love. I will also, no matter what, feel joy at the sight of white butterflies.

To his Godmother and Grandmother: You're both undeniably brilliant.

To the Boy on the Beach: You've been through so much worse than me, and you've come out of it much stronger and much, much, *much* prettier. You weren't always kind to me, but that's okay. You're a far better friend than you were a partner. I'm sorry I portrayed you unfavourably. It's sort of your fault for deciding to fuck a confessional writer who won't stop going on about her dead boyfriend. You were a vital, although incredibly painful, part of my recovery, and I'll always be grateful for that.

To DC: What else is there to say? Thank you for the happy memories. Thank you for your love and making me feel worthy of it. Thank you for the records, the pot-plants, and the shared conversations (especially the bitchy ones where I moaned about supposedly good writers. I will still always roll my eyes at Joyce.) Thank you for the feedback, both good and dismissive. Thank you for the way you spun me into something stronger. Thanks, actually, madly enough, for the trauma. If I were you, I'd say something really dark like "thank you for the writing material," but I'm not going to say that because it's too disrespectful (although I am, in my own sideways way, still saying it.) I still don't think this is fate. I still don't think this was meant to happen, that it's ultimately good, or that when god closes a door, he opens a window. This is still horrible. My tenuous flirting with religion has more to do with your personality and what you represented than how I actually feel. But it's happened now, and I might as well sift through the pieces you left for me and try to find a way for this to be okay. So thank you.

And I really loved you by the way.
Honestly, I did.

Cathy

(The Final Poem by DC)

We swapped our

bitten apples

at the station

　　　though

the tracks were

vacant.

You took my cards

touched my face

and asked if I was

real.

I ached when the

day became

its empty self

again.

I bit my apple.

　　　even though

it wasn't

real.

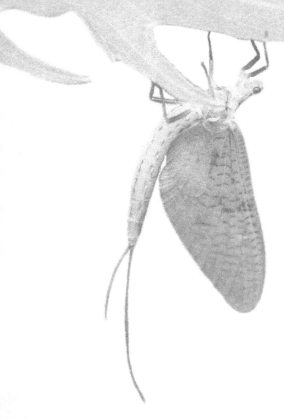

Introduction:

A Hypothetical Situation

At some point in your life, you'll find someone who loves you romantically. Hopefully, this love will be reciprocated. Happiness can be found within this shared affection.

Let's start with one couple. Let's say they begin as friends. Let's say that during a drunken night of Scrabble, music, and poetry, they kiss. They'll lie nose to nose in bed with eyes closed, feigning attempts at sleep, knowing that most friendships don't have sleepovers like this. She'll hear his shaking, nervous exhales and do nothing to push the situation forward. Later, she'll wonder why she did nothing, why she let him struggle knowing that he wanted to kiss her. The ruse will end, and he'll sit up, leaning on an elbow to say:

"I'm going to do a bad thing."

And when she answers:

"Are you going to kiss me, Dan Collins?"

He'll respond with:

"Let's talk logistics."

And in these relationships of mutual romantic attachment, the couple will go through good times and bad. Let's say they drink wine in student bars and cosy, underground pubs with no phone reception. Let's say they have snow days under blankets after struggling for hours to get home. Let's say he mixes tea and coffee, and they find that, actually, it tastes exactly as you'd expect a mixture of tea and coffee to taste. Let's say that when she's running late to university and texts to say she can't meet him for a drink, he pours her pint into a plastic bottle and brings it into the lecture hall. Let's say they have mutual friends who say things like:

"Here comes DC and Marvel," and they will gain new identities by morphing into one thing, iconic opponents feeding off each other's shared antipathy. Let's say they love each other, and they both fall quickly and deeply.

Let's say there are also difficult times. Let's say a relative close to Dan Collins attempts suicide. Let's say she overdoses on anti-depressants, and her organs begin to shut down. Let's say Dan Collins finds the body and, after ringing the ambulance and running through the absolute worst possibilities, the only person he's able to tell is his partner. Let's say she waits on the other side of a telephone while Dan Collins waits in the ICU, that whenever he rings it's with increasingly worse news, his voice sounding duller and emptier each time. Let's say that a different relative also falls drastically sick on the same day. She fits in front of him over the top of the other relative's overdosing organ-failing body (still lying unconscious in a hospital bed) and then needs a bed of her own. Let's say that all this happens in a matter of days, two weeks after the first kiss.

(At this point, reader, you may realise that the story is not fictitious. As fiction, it's so horrendous and confusing it would reach the point of being unbelievable. Regardless, this is all hypothetical. Hypothetically, thankfully, they both recover.)

Let's say he describes this trauma well—the finding of the blue-faced relative clutching at his photograph, mumbling incoherent apologies. Let's say DC is a disturbingly talented writer, and it shows in moments like these. Let's say that, despite his impressive ability to turn a phrase, to make each sentence sound like poetry, to describe feelings in such a way that it creates a physical sensation for the listener, he is also emotionally distant.

At some point in everyone's life, if they choose to develop a romantic relationship, they will also develop together some Mutual Friends. Friends that start off as singularly owned become shared. This network will grow stronger with time. As a group, they will create good memories. The couple will have an array of supportive friends to choose from, all of whom say lovely things like: "Here comes DC and Marvel!"

Let's say DC didn't want this support. Let's say he only wanted his partner to know anything about the situation and kept it secret from the rest. Let's say she felt pride and vindication, loved being in the role of the protector, but gradually grew to be increasingly concerned by the burden of this trauma. Let's say that after his relative's suicide attempt, a lifetime of suffering and poor mental health released itself as anger, insecurity, and pain, all directed entirely at his new partner, who couldn't say a word about the situation to any Mutual Friend, because it wasn't her situation to divulge.

Perhaps he was worried to let a good thing go; he knew that the relationship was positive, and so he reacted with fear and anger. Perhaps the relationship was not good, and he was deliberately trying to sabotage it subconsciously for his self-protection. Perhaps the relationship was a good thing, but copious amounts of self-loathing encouraged him to believe that he didn't deserve to have it, causing him to behave in a dangerous and aggressive way in order to prevent the good thing from continuing. We are, of course, just speculating. It's possible for all of these things to simultaneously be true.

Let's say he becomes very angry at his partner after he's had a few drinks.

Let's say a few drinks happen almost every night.

Let's say he becomes controlling.

Let's say he's jealous of any relationship his partner has, regardless of how platonic it may be.

Let's say his partner's mental health, work, study, familial relationships, friendships, and living situation suffer as a result of his behaviour, and she feels trapped and scared but unable to leave because who could possibly leave someone who's so recently experienced so much pain?

Let's say he changes his classes so that all of his seminars are with her.

Let's say after every seminar, he assumes he can stay at her house.

Let's say she stops having friends come up to visit because it always causes a fight.

Let's say, when she says no to him for anything, be it her time, her body, or her attention, he grows angry and manipulative, insisting on doing the thing anyway.

Let's say when she asks for a night off, he follows her home.

Let's say she is not allowed a break without it being seen as a sign of neglect.

Let's say that the burden of being his only emotional support becomes crippling.

Let's say he threatens suicide if she ever leaves him.

Let's say that he gets drunk and turns up at her house, shouting, refusing to leave until the police have to be called and statements have to be made.

Let's say that the relationship ends there in terms of mutuality.

Let's say she leaves him.

Let's say he stalks her.

Let's say he threatens self-harm more erratically the longer she stays away from him.

Let's say he sends ominous suicide threats to Mutual Friends in the hopes of encouraging her to contact him.

Let's say he is hospitalised from failed overdoses but convinces staff he is no longer a danger to himself.

Let's say she lives in constant fear that something terrible will happen, but constant disgust at the blatant attempts at manipulation.

Let's say he wants to die.

Let's say he threatens suicide.

Let's say he makes good on his threat.

Let's say the relationship lasted four months. Let's say that Dan Collins was twenty-two, and let's remember that he's never coming back. This situation was obviously never hypothetical. I clearly have no problem with creating emotional distance.

Now, suicidal relatives, aging grandmothers, angry fathers, school friends, best friends, Mutual Friends, all marvel at the partner, all staring, all demanding some explanation.

"How could you let this happen?"

"He loved you."

"He blamed you."

"He said it in his note to you."

"This is your fault."

"You left him."

"Heartbroken."

"How dare you?"

And amongst all the angry, drunken tears, mostly the partner's own, she will sense the tone of accusation from the sober relatives who are all saying:

"We don't want to blame anyone. We just want answers."

And there will be silence while everyone stares at the partner like she is some abstract art-piece, a shit smeared on a canvas, disgusting but somehow interesting, and finally she realises that being marvelled at is not always a positive experience, and the attention she has always craved can be cruel.

At what point did this stop being an everyday experience?

Well, here are your fucking answers.

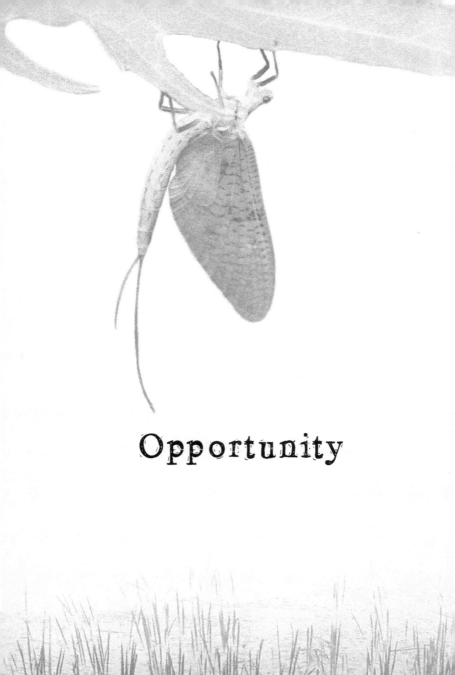

Opportunity

The Opportunity Rover died
On Mars
Alone
While it was getting dark
And his batteries were low.

And at the time,
I was reading
about Ziggy Stardust:
The man who fell to earth
and sacrificed himself
in reverent crucifixion.

And at the time
I was grieving
a beautiful young boy
who wrote stories about
Catholic guilt
repressing sexualities.

And I thought about how much this boy
loved David Bowie.
And I thought about the Spiders from Mars.
And I thought about rock and roll suicides,

But mostly,
I just worried about Opportunity
Because it is
So scary
In the dark.

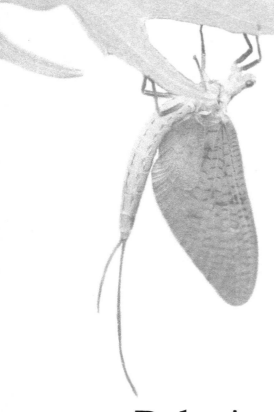

Delusional
Conversation #1

People speak about the five stages of grief so often it's become a cliché: denial, anger, bargaining, depression, acceptance...

"But I feel all these things all the time," I would think as I sat in front of Web MD wondering if self-diagnosis might help to create a sense of perspective.

Although, perhaps I didn't feel all the steps. I thought I'd skipped denial. In fact, if anyone tried to tell me I was in denial, I would have been irritated. Of course I knew he wasn't coming back because I wasn't a child or a moron, and I understood the concept of death. It was only many months later, after coming home from university, dissertation handed in and that chapter of my life firmly closed behind me that I realised that actually, this was never going to go away. Dan Collins was dead. There would always be his suicide and it would forever affect my life and the lives of those who loved him. I cried a lot when I got home. I cried more than I intended to.

I'm not a spiritual person. DC's suicide wasn't fate. It wasn't destined to happen, and it was completely without point. Dan Collins shouldn't have died. This wasn't a chapter of my life, but instead a large coffee stain spreading over the whole book, and sure the stain would eventually fade as the pages keep turning, but fundamentally the whole book was now crinkled and ruined and... (*what do you reckon, DC? Is this prose style okay? Am I doing alright? Perhaps I'm being too flippant and this isn't the time for a quirky, extended metaphor. Metaphors were always your territory, anyway. Like you said, they boost the word count.)*

DC would never get to write any more chapters about himself, metaphorical or otherwise. This was not a nice realisation.

Alongside the depression, I was also very angry. I've found that the stages of grief don't really work in neat little blocks, but overlap, and skip the queue, and beat each other up to try and get the most attention (*See? Metaphors again! I'm getting so self-assured now, it's embarrassing*). All the stages are terrible, but the worst one by far has been anger. I was bitter, hateful, utterly despicable and resentful of everyone around me. I'm not the best to be around anyway what with all my insecurity and defensive tendencies, but it multiplied ten-fold during the "anger" stage. Anger is yet another thing that simply hasn't gone away.

I'm conscious that right now I am bargaining. I know this because I wake up a lot in the middle of the night, and I don't go back to sleep. My thought patterns go a little like this: *If I could have him back for one day, we could have closure. If he descended now onto earth, I would show him how much I'd really loved him, I'd show everyone how much I'd really loved him, and no one could accuse me of being a cold, punishing, femme-fatale heartbreaker. He himself could explain how things were complex. It wasn't that I'd left him heartbroken and vulnerable, and it wasn't that he was an evil abuser; it was a combination of the two things mixed together with a lot of uncertainty, psychosis, and bad timing. This could all be fixed if I had him back for just one day.*

People refer to DC as "lovesick," often focusing on the "love" but not the "sick." When they do focus on the "sick," by virtue of feminist intentions or a counselling degree, they define the sickness as unhealthy and obsessive. They assume that the sickness overrides the love. In fact, the love is non-existent as made evident by the sickness. People argue that the fact his psychosis made him treat me so poorly shows that the love wasn't really legitimate, and I wonder if there can ever be such a thing as interpreting "lovesick" in a balanced kind of way. He was both sick, and he loved me. Can this not be the case? If this was true, we'd start again with different attitudes. We'd dedicate ourselves fully to each other, and there would always be love, alongside the sickness, and together we'd make it work.

I'm worried about the next stage. I don't think the next stage will have so many comforting fantasies.

I picture him sitting opposite me while I scribble this down on a disturbingly sunny February day. He's wearing sunglasses, and I have to squint to look at him.

"What are you doing?" he'd ask.

15

"Trying to figure out my feelings surrounding your death and the subsequent blame I feel," I'd reply.

"And is the wine necessary?"

"The wine is absolutely necessary."

I write this conversation in a coffee shop by the port of Santurtzi in the Basque Country where I recently moved to escape. It's beautiful here. In life, Dan Collins had never been abroad, and I think he might look impressed because one-on-one he often looked impressed in my direction. In a crowd, I seemed subpar and delusional around him, but one-on-one I felt spectacular

"And how are your feelings?" he might ask me.

"Better than they were before."

"So, what do you need to figure out?"

"I'm trying to figure out if you loved me."

I watch the figure opposite me glitch. Or more accurately, I imagine watching the figure opposite me glitch, as there isn't really a figure, and I'm being forced, even by my own imagination, to admit that this is a fantasy. I picture it like a holograph crackling in and out, black squares interrupting his face and body. I make the fantasy tell me what I want to hear.

"Of course I loved you. Deeply. You were the best and only person possible for me. I was very unwell, but none of this was your fault. I made my own decision. The guilt-trips, the blame, the suicide note, they were all mistakes. In this new, healthy mind-set in which you always picture me, I see you as faultless. Flawless. Completely innocent and loveable, and the affection I feel towards you was then, and still is, utterly pure."

"Very good," I'd say. "I love you too," then sip my wine and feel comforted.

This is what I need to hear and, for a brief moment, I've heard it. I would like the conversation to continue, but the problem is I have no idea what else I need him to say. I can't use my marionette madness to think up the poignant, intelligent, hilarious things he would have said in life, so I leave it here. All is well. Except I can't shake the feeling that the real DC would have explained it in a more beautiful way.

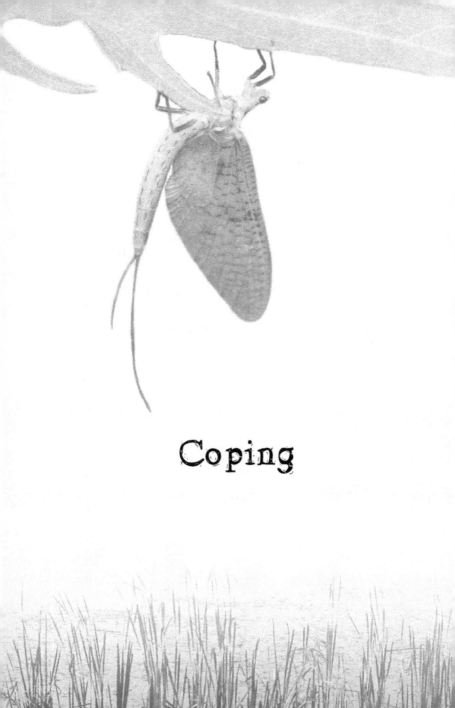

Coping

I woke up this morning

And he was dead

And I made my bed

And he was dead

And I had to start work soon

And he was dead

But first I did yoga

And he was dead

'Cause it's good to stay healthy

And he was dead

Then I took a hot shower

And he was dead

And I went off to work

And he was dead

And I added to star-charts

And he was dead

Because children need praise

And he was dead

Then we went out for drinks

And he was dead

And my colleagues told stories

And he was dead

About nightmare children

And he was dead

And how to control them

And he was dead

And I laughed along with them

And he was dead

And I kept on drinking

And he was dead

And I drank more than they did

And he was dead
Then I spoke about him and

    How he was dead

And my colleagues kept squirming

      And he was dead

Then they all went home

        And he was dead

But I couldn't walk back now

          And he was dead

So I thought I'd call Uber

            And he was dead

But my phone was dead too.

Oh no.

Jesusnopleasedon'tbedeadpleasenoImean
itdon'tbedeadyoucan'treallybedeadwhen
ImissyousomuchpleasenoI'lldoanything
tomakesureyoustopbeingdeadifIcanI'll-
tradeplacespleasedon'tbedeadwhen-
youknewI'dbeleftinastateonmyownIswear-
Ican'tkeepdoingthisbullshitdayinandday-

outthesameroutinepretendingit'sokay-
whenit'ssoexhaustingandpointlessandI-
can'tdoitanymorepleasedon'tbedeaddon'tbe-
deaddon'tbedeaddon'tbedeaddon'tbedead-
dontbedeaddontbedeaddontbedead.

Fuck
I'm so sorry
I was coping so well until this point.

Delusional
Conversation #2

There are a dozen smirky Basque teenagers in front of me doing an exercise on colour-based idioms.

He sees the world in black and white.

The note was a red herring.

His death came out of the blue.

Et cetera.

This was preceded by a brief reading about a Max Ernst forgery. I tried to get them interested in art for a few minutes, but they weren't interested, so they carried on being smirky. It's amazing the things that teenagers find ridiculous. Anyone with an opinion on anything is open game for mockery. They hate being here. They hate learning English, but you try to let them branch out into any other type of discussion, and they're confused and distrusting. They set their emotional guards up ten miles high, so that no one in the room could be convinced that they care about anything. We live a forty-five-minute drive away from Guernica.

"So, what other artists can we name?"

"…"

"There's a big memorial to one of them in the metro station here."

"Picasso."

"Brilliant! What art piece?"

"Guernica."

"And what is Guernica about?"

"…."

"What kind of art is it?"

"…"

"Is it realism? Self-portrait? Landscape? What do we think?"

"…"

"Okay, Let's look through our vocab…"

"Abstract."

"Good! Yes, abstract. Picasso is famous for the invention of Cubism. Let me find a good picture of... Good. Okay. So, what do we think?"

"…"

"Come on, what do we think? Do we like it?"

"Not really." This girl with her brown, curly hair is attempting to be bold and rebellious, but it will backfire. I'm still young and ridiculous enough to embrace any reaction to art as valid.

"Okay, great! Why not?"

They all try so hard not to catch your eye. You'd think I was interrogating them, which I suppose I am. She shrugs.

"I just don't."

Forget it.

"Fine. Page 105, vocabulary task, fill in the blanks. I'm going to give you five minutes, then we'll run through the answers."

There's visible relief in the room, although they hate English tasks. Had I not attempted to speak to them they would've rolled their eyes and moaned at being made to write, but something about my pathetic attempt to engage with them means they now have a new perspective, and anything is fine provided they don't have to share their opinion. I understand as I'm writing this how naïve I sound. A seasoned secondary-school teacher would laugh me out the door. Obviously seventeen-year-olds don't care about abstract art. But this is where I begin to miss academia and other students around me fighting over each other to speak about their personal views on Guernica. I want to go back and study, but I'm not quite clever or centred enough yet and, anyway, it wouldn't be the same as the MA was because I'd miss *you*, DC. Stupidly. I'd miss your pencil shavings and the way you'd connect everything with a tenuous link to Freud. I'd miss being giddy from pre-seminar drinks and that smirking face of yours (because make no mistake, it was still a smirk, the insufferable sign of all students, Basque or otherwise).

You would make some funny remark about aiming to reach word-count by exhausting metaphors. (And God, if you could see the absolute train-wreck of a metaphor I used earlier about coffee stains and trauma, your highlighter pen would be going mad.) In seminars, you'd always make comments which allowed you to remain kooky and facetious. It worked. People thought you were hysterical, and you were hysterical. I'm not making your charm apparent on the page. You would be able to, but I can't explain it well enough, and I'm making you seem a little difficult and pretentious, and maybe you were, but fucking hell, who wasn't? I appreciate you listening to me, and now I have non-begrudgingly admitted that I miss you, I want to ask you something else:

"Dan Collins, how do you feel about Guernica?"

"I don't know," you answer—because I don't know either and wouldn't want to be presumptuous. "Let's move on from Guernica. No one cares about Guernica."

"I care about Guernica!"

"No one else does. Move on."

"So, who is your favourite artist then?"

"I don't know, Cathy. We dated for four months and didn't really talk about art. Your interest in all things artistic began after I died and you were doing that dissertation on body fluids, which by the way wasn't as good as the hypothetical dissertation I would have written, but the amount of time you'd put in to polish it would grant you a slightly higher mark, and I'd make sure you knew you were exceptional for that."

"Thank you, Dan Collins."

"Let's talk about poets instead."

"Which poet?"

"I think Ted Hughes,"

"Oh no,"

"And Sylvia Plath."

"Oh Christ, don't make me think about this."

"I loved Hughes."

"I know you did. Your mum made you that crow badge, and you wore it on your jacket. It was very sweet."

"You didn't like him."

"That I did not, Dan Collins."

"And why was that?"

"I suppose I partially blamed him for the suicide of my favourite poet Sylvia Plath who I considered to be a much larger talent."

"Well."

"I do see the irony now, yes."

"And how do you feel about Ted Hughes these days?"

"Differently, I suppose. I still don't feel as strongly towards him as I do towards Plath who I'm convinced is a genius, but that's okay, isn't it? It's okay to have favourites, and it's okay to find nature poems kind of dull."

"And what did you do in your class last week?"

"Which class?"

"This is a conversation with yourself, baby-doll. I'm just here as a therapeutic exercise. You know exactly what class I'm talking about, although I appreciate the way you're exhausting the word count unnecessarily here."

"I would never call myself baby-doll."

"But I did, and I bet you miss it, you sentimental piece of shit."

"Well, I would definitely call myself a sentimental piece of shit, so fine. I remember the class. I remember I wrote a poem called 'Coping' where I repeated the line about you being dead repeatedly."

"Why did you do that?"

"To emphasise that no matter what you're doing or how mundane it is, death is never really out of your mind, especially after you've lost someone."

"And…"

"As a way of turning it into a mantra, reaching the point of breathlessness and panic towards the end. I know you always approved of repetition. It seemed appropriate."

"And you were attempting to echo…"

"Hughes. And his fucking poem in *Crow* where he constantly repeats the word 'death.' Fine, you got me. I guess I relate to Hughes now instead of the brilliant, genius, perfect, confessional goddess Sylvia Plath. But I would never have cheated on you. I would never have undermined your writing as he did hers. I'd definitely never have slept with a student because it's far too cliché, and anyway mine are seventeen and boring and don't care about Guernica."

"Where are your students, by the way? The exercise only took them five minutes to complete, and now they're all staring at you. I should probably go."

"Please don't."

"You're not much of a teacher, are you?"

"Fuck teaching."

"Come on, baby-doll. It's been time for me to go for a while now."

"Oh, fine…"

So you go. And I miss you, again. When I finally stand up, the class is irritated. I don't think they appreciated the break as much as I did.

"So, what about the first one?"

"…"

"Shall I pick someone at random?"

"…"

"Oihane."

"He beat her black and white."

"Yeah, you know what? Fine."

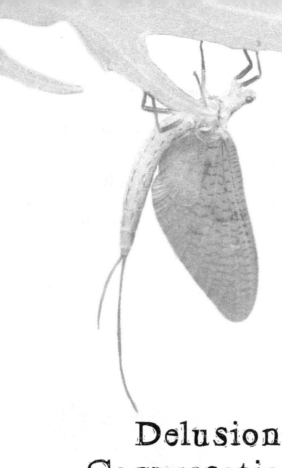

Delusional Conversation #3:

A letter, an apology, for the books.

It's getting painful to write again, DC. It's getting like how it was before. The sadness was something I could cling onto, and a part of me found it helpful and cathartic, but now I'm wishing it had never happened, that I'd never met you, and it could all just go away. I don't like myself very much, DC. I don't like myself at all.

Some pickpockets stole your book, DC. You left me a huge pile of Virginia Woolf books, and for so long I kept them in a neat line on a bookshelf next to where I worked. I would teach English lessons on my laptop and look over at them. If I had a break to write, I could flick through them and remember. Then I moved to the Basque Country and took a few with me. My bag was stolen with *To the Lighthouse* inside alongside my phone with all my pictures of you and our conversations. Some are saved online; some are burned into my memory. The best pictures were the ones I never took, but the ones I still remember when I close my eyes. An example:

The Best Picture

I'm leaning out of my second-storey window to shout down at you. I heard you ring the doorbell seconds before. I call you Dan Collins (always in full), and I tell you to come in. I'm joking around, but what I say I can't remember and is probably of no importance anyway. You wear a denim jacket and a beanie hat, and you look up at me and grin with perfect, straight, white teeth. I think "he looks like he's in love with me." I wonder if I look like I'm in love with you too.

But the phone is still gone, and the book disappeared. Then the others, the ones left on the shelf, were carelessly given away. My mother—(and I call her that because you always called your mum "Mother," and it always seemed so strangely Norman Bates-y, so creepy and Freudian, which of course fit your whole aesthetic perfectly. I remember the occasion this came up. It was a passing comment about accents. People in Birmingham say "Mom"; everyone else says "Mum." When asked what you say, you replied, perfectly deadpan, "I call my mother 'Mother'. And she calls me 'Cunt,'" and a Mutual Friend of Great Importance laughed so hard that people from other tables turned to stare in disapproval)—well, my mother gave the books away accidentally, and now they're not on any bookshelf I can reach. They're not at her house. They're not at my home. They mysteriously disappeared, but they're somewhere, DC. Everyone swore that they'd find them because they must be somewhere. But people stopped looking. Then my mother said that maybe they never existed, and if I couldn't remember exactly how many you'd given me, then perhaps they were never at home to begin with. Maybe I was losing my mind. I don't think so, though. I don't think I imagined those books.

At the time, I was fucking apoplectic. I've never been so full of hatred. I cried so much I couldn't breathe until I gagged on air, which is embarrassing to think about, although I was alone, but at the time, I thought of nothing but the pain. I couldn't see, DC. My eyes swelled up so drastically it looked like I had painful allergies. I only remember the feeling. It felt like you had died again.

I think you meant to punish me, DC. I know I'm cynical. I don't believe in afterlife or god, or judgement, or anything like that. I used to lie a lot as a child and say that I saw ghosts, but I didn't really believe in them either. I know that when I dream about you and my counsellor says, "Do you think he was talking to you through your dream?" I will respond with something like, "No, I think I'm traumatised and it's coming out in my subconscious, giving me nightmares and insomnia," and then my counsellor will know that I believe in science and rational explanations, and for some reason, that will make me feel superior. This is something I used to be proud of, DC, but now it's a pain in my arse, DC, because if only I wasn't so stubborn in my atheism and my lack of spirituality, I could have really believed that every time I saw a butterfly, it was you coming to visit me, and that you really did speak to me through dreams.

Somehow though, it seems like the certainty of my culpability is still stronger than my usual rationality because I think you stole my bag, DC, and got rid of my books to punish me. The night my bag was stolen, I was drinking and I met someone. He seemed very kind, DC. I liked his shitty hand tattoo, and he'd studied English too, DC, and I made sure to hug him goodbye really tightly, and then my bag was gone.

The police found it later. Only the phone and the book were missing. Everything else was intact. I think that you took them, DC. I think you decided that these things belonged to someone who was more deserving. I don't think you were wrong to take them from me. I think, realistically, I needed reminding of my priorities.

I don't know what to do if I'm not a martyr. I don't really know how to be successful or happy anymore. I'm not sure about anything except the fact that I am really, truly sorry. I understand that letters, pictures, books, and records, all these things won't bring you back. If I memorise the suicide note, it doesn't stop you from dying. Nothing I do to honour your memory matters in the slightest. There was a time, close after your death, when all I wanted was to forget you, but now I get so terrified that one day I won't remember that image of you smiling up at me that sometimes I think about taking up painting just so that I can immortalise those few seconds while I still can. I'd paint it and I'd examine every detail intensely. But I'm no artist, and worse, I'm impatient. I'd draw you as a stickman and it wouldn't be the same. Maybe, these words will help to immortalise you. If only I was a better writer. I wish that I could do your memory some justice.

But no, for once I'm going to be nice about myself. There are some benefits that come alongside writing with clarity. Sometimes your stories were difficult to follow. I remember when I met your mother ("Mother") for a drink, and we spoke about your latest piece, and she had found it difficult to get through. I described your work as "opaque," and she said that was a good term, and I sensed pride radiating from you. I was confident for once, which now feels strange. I used to make comments on your prose when we offered each other feedback and I would say things like, "This is good, but can you make it more accessible?" I didn't realise at the time that I was staring in the face of something genius.

Was it really genius though, DC? Do I only think that because you're dead now? But no. There really was something tangible about the quality and execution of your writing. You were legitimately talented, and that is not the indulgence of a grieving ex-girlfriend.

But for some conceited reason, I felt equal to you back then. You had your style; I had mine. Now I'd never dare say anything negative about your work. Now I read your pieces, and it's like every word is set down with purpose and perfection. Others knew. Our Mutual Friend of Great Importance spoke about you, even when you were alive, as someone extraordinarily talented. This same friend let me know you thought very little of my work too, and since this is a letter, I will shamelessly beg you to tell me if what he said had any truth in it at all...

Silence.

Well, this conversation is more one-sided than the others. Perhaps you can tell me how you feel in a dream, and I'll later dismiss it as superstition. When you were alive, I'd belittled the mutual admiration between you and our Mutual Friend of Great Importance as some boy's club, Joyce-bumming, white-male-writer mentality that I had absolutely no interest in. I was wrong. You were both more switched-on than I was in noticing true originality.

But, despite the rambling, there is something good about my writing. I say things honestly. You would describe me beautifully, I'm sure, but it would be in code, with puns and inside jokes that would be difficult to decipher. You would use Freudian slips to insinuate eroticism. It would be highbrow. It would be modernist. But I, however clumsily, will tell the truth.

The denim jacket was blue. The beanie hat was burgundy. Your jeans were black. Your teeth looked very white. Your eyes were dark brown to the point that you always described them as "black." Gillet Road, the shitty street I lived on, was full of litter. There were two pot-plants on the windowsill, and I sucked in my stomach to lean over them. The plants had sticky notes on them. One said: "I'm watching you, Cathleen," and then on the other: "Roses are red / Violets are (yes, I think) blue / Cathleen / I am still watching you." It was a very funny inside joke. I had no idea why you bought me pot-plants, but the sentiment was sweet. You were handsome. I think you were never more handsome than in those few seconds. I remember your smile. I remember being ridiculously attracted to you, and I think that my heart probably experienced some sense of "dropping" or "yearning," but this is getting far too unclear now.

Is that enough to immortalise you? Have I done enough? I wish that every second we spent together could be described like this and remembered as clearly. Memories are so disgustingly unreliable.

You're fading, DC. There's not much that I can do about this. I feel terrible and I want you to be here, and I think that's why I get hysterical whenever I lose books or photographs, whenever I'm unsure about what the suicide note really said, or what it was you told me on the phone that time. You shouldn't already be finished and completed, DC. You should still be alive to grow and build more memories. You should be a work in progress. There's nothing more anyone can gain from you, so the least I can do is not lose the fragments of you I have left.

So DC, this is an apology. I'm sorry I'm so clumsy. I'm sorry that I have the tendency to break, drop, and lose things. I'm sorry I was so careless with the memories you left me. I'm sorry I didn't meet you for coffee during that last month when you were psychotic, and I'm sorry that I left you in such a terrible state.

I wish I was one of those mourners who wore black veils and carved your name into my forearm. I should be in a hospital on suicide watch doing nothing except crying for you. I shouldn't be in Bilbao flirting with boys with shitty hand tattoos and getting my satchel stolen. I shouldn't be leaving your things at my parents' house hoping that they'll be safe on my return. But this is who I am, and I am sorry. I'm sorry I'm clumsy. I'm sorry I'm resilient. I'm sorry that I've made mistakes. I'm sorry that I did the right thing. I'm sorry that I met you. I'm sorry that I didn't stay with you for longer. I am full of contradictions with no idea about whether what I did was right or wrong, but one thing I'm overwhelmingly sure of is that I'm really, really, undoubtedly sorry.

And that this apology matters as little as the books did.

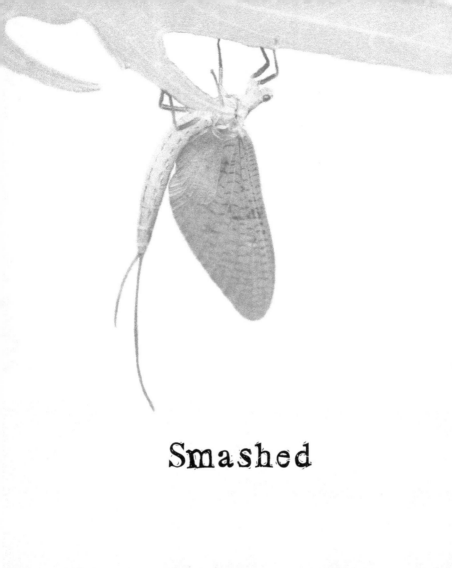

Smashed

Mug shatters
on a kitchen floor.

I check my hand,
still shaking,
still uncertain just like always.
Just like stupid
Clumsy
Just like

Yes now,
I remember
aged ten, scalded,
hands red spotted,
Coffee on white carpet flooring,
God, I was just so annoying.
I remember
screams of anger.
Dabbing towels
and burning palms
and peeling skin between my fingers.

Cracks in porcelain
are endearing.
That's what people say.
A testament

to authenticity,

sincerity, simplicity,

but all I can remember is

the way they made my mouth bleed.

But this is all my fault.

Why pick up something fragile with
shaking hands

And punctured thoughts?

I guess the chips don't matter now.

I guess it's all just fragments now.

For sure, the mug is nothing, shattered,

I am shattered too.

And if it's smashed

Then I suppose

That I'll get smashed again.

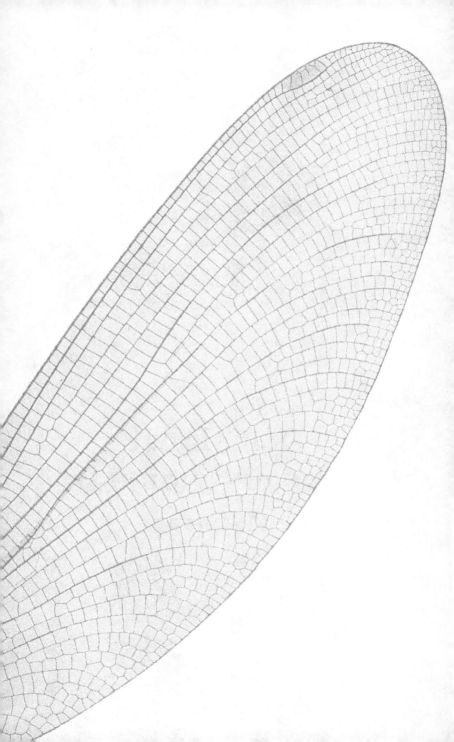

Delusional
Conversation #4:
Mapping

My sense of direction is so poor that I don't recognise places I've already been to because if the situation is different, the feelings and associations are different, and therefore, to my mind, it cannot be the same place. I'm in the same classroom twice a week but with two different groups of students. The students change things. They make the room seem large or small, dark or light, cramped or spacious. It isn't just to do with them. Wednesdays at 10:15 don't *feel* like Mondays at 8:45. There's a taste I associate with Mondays that isn't there for Wednesdays. Mondays feel a greenish colour; Wednesdays feel orange. I don't know how this makes sense, but it does. In my memory, that room is two distinctly separate places, which may as well be at opposite ends of the universe. Spatial awareness is something I fail at spectacularly, alongside self-awareness, perspective, and writing concisely in order to reach a point.

Manchester airlines have hostesses with crooked teeth. I like that. I appreciate beauty as much as anyone else, but I prefer endearing flaws. They're comfortable. I particularly enjoy crooked teeth because my own teeth are so wide and gappy. That crookedness seems thousands of miles away from what I am, and that makes it alien and beautiful. Coming home, I obviously recognise that England is the same, but it doesn't feel like that. I want to make it clear that this isn't because of my own personal growth. This isn't because now I've travelled and seen the world, the place seems *smaller*, like I've outgrown it, or any of those other frustrating things people say when they've just finished a gap-year and decided to embrace narcissism. It's just a different situation, a different feeling, ergo, a different place.

I did my usual lap of the bedroom in the attic of my parents' house. I kissed your photograph. I hugged the shirt you left me. I read your suicide note.

I didn't take any of these things with me when I moved because I wanted to have a "fresh start." Ridiculous. Long ago, we established that life isn't like chapters in a book. *(Do you remember, DC? The awful coffee stain metaphor?)* It's not like you can turn a page and there's a whole blank canvas to write on. *(Oh look, I'm needlessly continuing.)* Days bleed together like music genres, and perhaps at some point you might notice how one genre is different to another, but the original influences are still there because nothing could have grown and existed without what has gone before it to influence the change. *(This is not an original concept, I know, but bear with me; it's an extended metaphor for life. I think the palpable success of the chapter metaphor has stuck with me.)* What's more: people don't just stop listening. They're still there, these genres, still being played in depressed teenagers' bedrooms while they wish they'd been born in the past. They're still being picked up by new bands who will cite the legends as influencers.

I give you this muddled and convoluted analogy as I stare at my box of records, considering the David Bowie ones you left me. I wonder if I have time to play them, realise that it's too late, that I'd wake people up, that it's perhaps not sensible anyway. David Bowie still exists. Dan Collins, you still exist. My life in the Basque Country isn't a fresh start because these things will always exist no matter where I go. I'll always have the same feelings, the same confusion, the same trauma. The best I can hope for is that it becomes easier to handle. The best I can hope for is that some depressed teenager might start a band and write a song inspired by you and you'll live forever.

I've already said that I'm not growing much, and there's some obvious truth to that. I'm isolating myself and becoming cruel. I'm drinking too much, and I'm no longer trying hard to be better, to be authentically myself. Instead, I'm settling on being normal, on being liked, which is ridiculously difficult by the way. It's apparent during all my stilted conversations with my perfectly lovely co-workers that I'm failing abysmally.

I sit in my old bedroom holding onto a suicide note, drunk, having wasted an extraordinary amount of money on plane wine. I hoped it would be enough to allow me to cope with seeing my family after they lost your books. I am still so angry at them and so guilty about the anger. Negative emotions beget negative emotions; self-loathing begets loathing begets self-loathing etc. Alcohol seemed like the best solution. Now, I'm woozy and alone.

"What do I do, imaginary Dan Collins?"

"The answer's in your hands," you respond. "I told you in the note."

"Keep on going as I'm going?"

"Exactly."

"But I'm not sure, DC. I don't think going as I'm going is a good thing to do. I'm often so deeply unhappy."

"And you're often contented too."

"True, but I always wonder if I'm ever really happy. As in intrinsically, sincerely happy with who I am as a person. How can I be sure that I'm doing the right thing and living the right life?"

"I don't think worrying neurotically about whether you're truly happy or not is the answer. Agonising about this is a sure-fire way to make all organic happiness disappear."

"You're right. Happiness is like an orgasm…"

"In that you miss sharing it with me."

"So, this is it then. I keep on going as I'm going. I'll stop worrying about whether I'm really happy."

"And also you should stop drinking so much and doing drugs at festivals because you promised my mother that you wouldn't ever do drugs when she texted you to ask if you'd gotten me hooked on opioids prior to my suicide."

"Yeah, that sounds pretty reasonable. You offer such brilliant advice, Dan Collins."

"Oh, but this is nothing to do with me, baby-doll. I wouldn't ever tell you to engage in less hedonism. That goes against everything I ever stood for. I made my own pathetic attempts to see counsellors, but really, I indulged in the glorified idea that mental illness just demon-strated passion and strength of character. All my attempts at self-improvement were really just to keep you happy so that you wouldn't consider leaving me for better, more emotion-ally stable options. At least in my own, psy-chotic brain that's how I perceived it. It's still surprising that I told you to 'keep going on as you're going.' I even encouraged you to find others who might love you. That kind of level-headedness was so out of character for me. I guess it shows the depths of my under-standing. Or maybe it was a way to relieve the guilt about killing myself and blaming you. Maybe the well-wishes were utterly insincere. Maybe I thought that if I sent you enough compliments and kind regards, then no one would see me as manipulative. You could then be firmly confirmed as a cold, abusive bitch. I could still have had every intention of you ignoring my kind regards and joining me in the void of nothingness. Although, that seems cynical even for you. I don't think I ever really wanted you to die. Realistically, it's probably less complicated. It's probably that it seemed like the right thing to say at the time. But either way, this entire speech is from you. It's your brain, your ideas. You're not even attempting to emulate my voice because the convoluted quirkiness I developed is incredibly difficult to emulate. This is a messy over-analysis. This is all you, baby-doll."

"Okay, thank you for all of that, imaginary Dan Collins," I continue. "If this is true, then I am incredibly proud of my self-awareness, and also angry that I refuse to follow my own advice."

"Well, who's to say it's even good advice? Now we've established that you're talking to yourself, it seems natural you think your own way of doing things sounds intelligent and sensible. Maybe both of us are getting all of this wrong and the correct solution is to hang yourself from the skylight right now, or to find a nice cult to join, or to run away to Tibet to live as a monk and embrace the sensations of ice-cold pain from the top of a mountain."

"Oh God, you're right. Now everything's uncertain again."

"Or, for once, instead of worrying about your own advice which you will forever have doubts about, you could follow mine instead."

"So, keep on going as I'm going?"

"Exactly. This conversation seemed circular and unnecessary. Yet again, I'm glad to see you unnecessarily exhausting a word-count."

"But it's so hard to keep on going when you have no idea what direction you're going in or where exactly you'll end up."

"Oh, baby-doll, come on now. That shouldn't matter at all. When have you ever been good with directions?"

The issue with
delusional
conversations

The fact is, he wouldn't say any of these things. I'm sure he'd say something quite sweet if I saw him again, but I'm also sure he'd say something manipulative alongside it. In reality, although of course this could never be reality, the conversation would be more like the suicide note or the final phone-call that I hadn't known would be the final phone-call. This was after the first suicide attempt. I didn't tell him I loved him; I just asked him where I needed to send the ambulance. I think I hammered home that I wasn't impressed, that I felt his actions were controlling, and his expressions of love unwanted. What a wonderful thing to remember about yourself. Of course, now I would tell him I love him. Now, I would tell him that every day.

The question is though, would I suggest to other people that they change tack? Would I tell another twenty-two-year-old girl to confess their undying adoration for the abusive ex-boyfriend on the end of the phone who'd swallowed thirty pills and wouldn't tell anyone where he was? No. Of course I wouldn't.

It doesn't make the shame fade though. It doesn't make the doubts any clearer.

Here is something I'm sure Dan Collins would say if I could see him one more time:

"I just want to tell you that I love you. You, you perfect sweet angel. This is all because I can't cope without you, and no one else will compare, so this is all your fault because…"

Or something. Obviously, he'd say it more articulately. Articulacy was a very apparent skill of his.

I often think about the police officer who left me the voice message after Dan Collins' first disappearance. "We're ringing you because we've been informed that you're the cause…" *Cause.*

I remember his mother ("Mother") storming into my house during his disappearance, saying that if he was dead she'd kill me because it would be my fault. And then the note:

"I know I met my future in you and when that emptied so did I."

The police officer, the mother, and the man himself. Three people, at least, who hold me accountable. Then there are those who read the article which held me accountable too. The relationship was described as "intense" — accurate, but still an unfair assessment of my behaviour. Now, I'm writing this stupid book. I understand well that if anyone reads it, I'll be subjecting myself to further scrutiny. I'm conscious that my one-sided depictions of people are potentially cruel and unfair. This may all be horrendously immoral. Is it worth it for the sake of a therapeutic exercise? Probably not. Ah well.

I'm writing this in pencil. That matters. Most of the time I write first drafts in pen with scribbles and messes and dots. Dan Collins wrote in pencil. He had a sharpener on his desk and the shavings always stained the classroom table. Every word had to be retractable. The first draft must be flawless on the page— perfect, fluent sentences with no mess, and I envy this. I miss him. It's apparently possible to feel both irritation and affection towards the same behaviour. This whole experience is teaching me that mutually exclusive things somehow always coexist.

So, while I'm embracing a lack of logic, let me picture these delusional conversations. Let me imagine that my pillow is his chest on nights when I can't sleep, let me fantasise I plucked his psychosis away, and that my daydreams are not so far from the reality. Let's say that with his mind clear, he would say the things I want to hear.

Yes, I did love you.

This was never your fault.

You did everything you could, and I want you to be happy.

Keep on going as you're going.

I wonder if in doing this I'm still in denial. I wonder if I'm a hypocrite, living within delusions while claiming to be an advocate for sanity. I wonder a lot of things, but this concern right now is not at the top of the list.

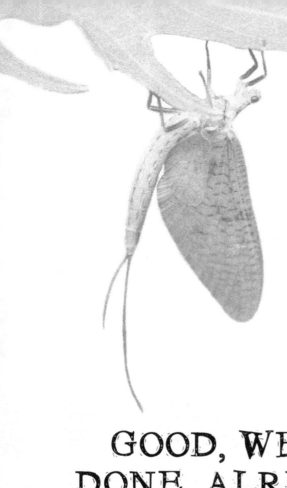

GOOD, WELL
DONE, ALRIGHT,
CALM DOWN.

They told us to write about a heist.
But I wanted to write about
A suicide pact.

I met them in the middle and watched
Thelma and Louise
Focused on the scene
Straight after the robbery
Where they're laughing in the
Thunderbird
'Cause there, they were alive.

You marked the story for me,
Stapled it, professionally.
You scribbled in the margin,
And highlighted the text.
I know you never said
But I could tell you weren't impressed.
You liked the suicide though
Scribbled, "yes, yes, yes, yes, yes."

My darling,
I'm glad you found the words
well-crafted.
I never meant for you to take them,
As an instruction manual.

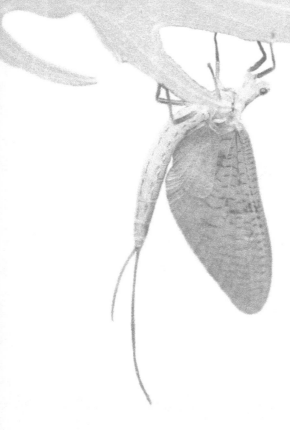

Kill Your Darlings

One day, I hope to become a better editor. Right now, I'm horrible at it. I cling onto bad sentences, scared to let them go even though they're sabotaging an entire story because there's a part of me which thinks maybe there's some core-truth in those jarring, clumsy phrases. I've wasted so much of my life polishing dirt. This is mostly an academic concern, but it can also apply to my personal life. I'm often told by my very loving, and yet emotionally stunted, family members that I cling onto negativity while ignoring all the good things, (although I'm told this by the people I generally consider to be negative, which either completely confirms their point or dismisses their opinion entirely). I think they're probably right, though. There's something self-flagellating in my behaviour, which perhaps explains my interest in this Christ-like, Catholic, guilt-ridden, choir-boy I write about so extensively.

For the most part, I can memorise Dan Collins' suicide note.

"Cathleen,

I will be brief

Firstly, I say to you don't be angry or sad. It's easier to say than do."

After that things start to get muddled.

Something something immeasurable talent, *something something* conviction to do the right thing *something something something*.

I will do what I do (Black shoe? Plath?) because I believe I met my future in you and when that emptied
so did I.
Thank you for briefly being mine.
Dan Hubert Collins
(a mayfly.)

I'm disgusted with myself whenever I try to recite it as I fall asleep, and I find that I'm forgetting the words. At my parents' house, I would go back to the same black leather notebook with the slot in the back, and read it again and again and again, and every time I'd realise how much more beautiful and concrete his words were compared to my paraphrasing.

There was another sentence: "I'm sure I'm not alone in believing you are an extraordinary woman," but it's only intense practice which allows me to remember that. I always drew a blank at the adjective. What was it he called me? Phenomenal, was it? Exceptional? Exciting? No, *extraordinary*. Why is it always the compliments I forget? It seems like any indication of his love and affection I write off as a clear sign of his psychosis, whereas anything he said that hurt me is singed into my brain, never to be forgotten, to be screamed internally every time I think I might have some self-worth. The truth is what hurts you. It's better to live with an uncomfortable truth than a comfortable lie. Suffering builds character. In clinging onto terrible things, I am becoming a better person. Et cetera.

This is all justification for my ridiculous masochism, and I know this, and my university counsellor knows this, and my friends and family are sick of this, I'm sure. I've never been one for delicate cuts on wrists or straightener burns on my thighs, although I did dabble as an angsty teen with the conventional methods of self-harm. Instead, I pick at skin and tear off scabs. I cause scarring by digging into blackheads. The pain is less intense and much more subconscious, and I suppose that's part of the appeal. The biggest form of self-sabotage is this refusal to edit away my terrible sentences. I run through the same ones over and over again. I remember every time I could have said something kinder, every time he held me accountable for *his* actions, every time anyone has indicated that I am anything less than perfect.

Dan Collins called me talented often. When I received good grades the first semester, he bought me a card calling me a genius, and it was very sweet. I didn't sense any jealousy or bitterness—only affection and that, I think, is rare. In the suicide note, he reminded me that I had talent. "Immeasurable" talent in fact. We read each other's work and praised it constantly. It's a strong possibility that, with all of this evidence considered, Dan Collins may have thought I was a passable writer.

After the break-up, a Mutual Friend of Great Importance (whose approval I desperately craved, perhaps even more than Dan Collins') took Dan Collins out for a few drinks to ensure that he was coping okay with his newfound singledom. Supposedly, this was a horrendous night which consisted of many attempts to swallow pills which our Mutual Friend of Great Importance dragged away from Dan Collins disapprovingly. DC then escaped. Mutual Friend of Great Importance spent a small fortune on taxis tracking him down before DC eventually surrendered and agreed to come home from the cold. There was indigestible, low-grade alcohol involved. Apparently, he seemed a lot more psychotic than usual. Our Mutual Friend hid this from me until after the death, which was kind of him. I suppose he wanted to protect me.

Although, maybe not. I tend to think that Mutual Friend of Great Importance had no interest in protecting me because after his death he let me know in no uncertain terms what Dan Collins really thought.

"He said something about how I was lucky not to date a writer because apparently you can't tell them your true opinion of their work, or something? Like you can never be honest if you think they're completely talentless? I dunno. I don't know what he meant by that."

From the look in our Mutual Friend of Great Importance's eyes, I could tell that for one, he absolutely did understand what Dan Collins had meant by that, and two, he'd told me this because he wanted to hurt me. And that's all that matters now, isn't it? That's the uncompromising truth.

I want to get better at editing because that one thing DC said ruined the whole of my confidence and my trust in the fact that we had respect for each other and our own forms of artistic expression. I really did think he was brilliant. I liked the Freudian themes, and the purple prose, and the Nabakovian talent he had prior to even reading Nabokov. But he was, in many ways, insincere, often pandering to what others wanted, what they would feel happy to hear him say. I suppose he pandered to me too. He *must* have pandered to me.

I use too many clichés and the emotional distance I create is often dull. Repetition can get boring, and I suppose what some see as "unflinching" others see as "cringe-inducing." I send off first drafts too quickly because I'm excited to hear feedback. What's ironic is that this whole tangle of insecurity and self-loathing can be best expressed through the very popular cliché (and clichés, we are dutifully taught, should be edited away): The truth hurts.

Is this masochism or am I being brutally honest with myself? Am I self-indulgingly throwing away the positive so I can dwell further in self-pity, or am I accepting the reality of DC's perception of me? It's possible he made a comment to Mutual Friend of Great Importance about disliking my work because he disliked some, but not all, of it and at the time that's what he wanted to focus on. It's possible he liked all of it but was bitter about the break-up and in the midst of a mental collapse. But I remember the condescension with cold clarity, the way he sometimes laughed when offering suggestions, the information that he withheld from me about my work until he tore it apart in front of seminar groups, and I remember that around others he had never seemed that impressed by me. But he would brag about my grades to everyone if I wasn't there. Was it awe, or disbelief that such tosh had been graded so highly?

This whole section could be edited down to half the word-count but sod it, self-improvement can be found another day. One day, I might edit this project into something readable. I can't promise I'll do it well though.

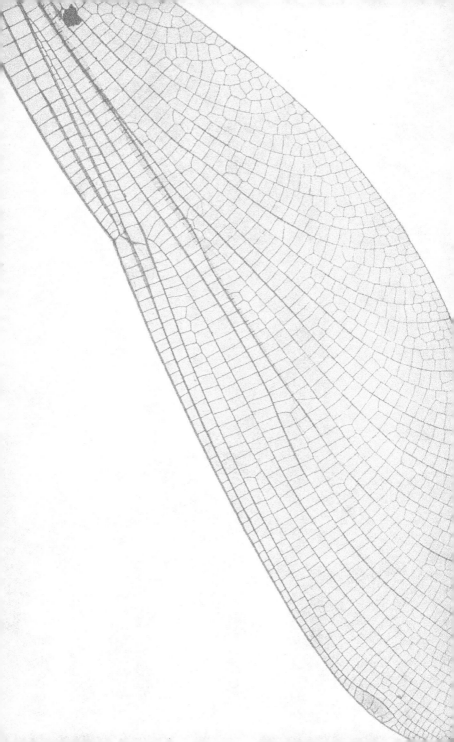

Apples

We shared an apple once.

It broke me

Pinkish flesh caught in my throat

I couldn't swallow

So I choked

I coughed until my nose streamed

My mascara smudging into me

And this was all your fault, of course

Because you made me laugh.

My love, you'd have me in hysterics

Even when I couldn't breathe.

With silence settled all around me

Biting into something weak

I'd rather eat myself than scream

So teeth-marks scarred my
knuckles white

But I don't laugh much anymore
now, do I?

And while I'm in this purgatory

Between alive and dead

And failing to communicate with both

You left me something comforting to help
me understand.

And you

wrote to me

about apples.

Fuck your apples

And fuck the fact you didn't use a
rhyme-scheme.

And fuck the way it worked
despite the lack

And fuck the fact I reckon it was done in
fifteen minutes

And fuck the way you're never
coming back.

Fuck this inconsistency,

And fuck this broken pen,

Fuck the citrus in my stomach

Fuck your apples yet again

Fuck this breathlessness

My lack of ease

Your cold cadaver

My weak knees

But mostly

Fuck your apples.

They mean nothing to me now.

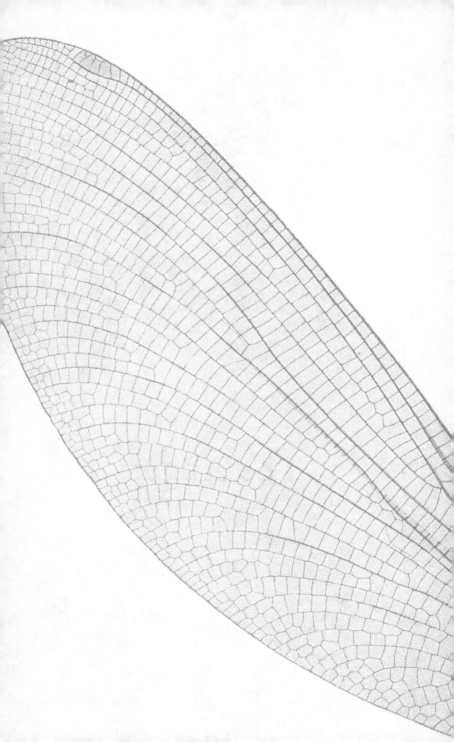

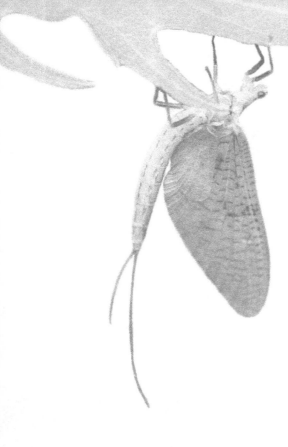

The Anger

It always comes back eventually. It doesn't take anything really. Someone will say he was talented, which he was and they're right to remember it, and jealousy shoots through me like an electric shock. People wouldn't say this about me if I died. They'd say different, but probably equally nice, things. That doesn't feel like enough, though. I want them to think of my writing as they thought of his, as though it were of the utmost importance, as though only through my words could I demonstrate the depth of my genius, but people won't say this about me because it isn't true.

I'm aware that this jealousy is a hideous part of me. I'm aware of the multitudes of hideous parts of me.

Dan Collins wasn't drawn to me because of a sense of shared, creative talent. He had an emotional need for companionship and a physical urge for human contact, and it isn't insulting that he fancied me because of this instead of because of a non-existent skill for penning stream-of-consciousness narratives. It's okay if people don't like me because of my creativity, and instead because I try to be a kind person in my own awkward, stumbling way. I know logically I'd rather date a kind person than a poet, although historical evidence may suggest otherwise. Still, I can't help it. The anger returns, insisting that it show itself on my face and in my demeanour.

Something that fires up the anger could be a video shared by a relative about the suicide epidemic amongst young men. They're right to do this. It's an important topic to bring to peoples' attention. Angry, hurt men are dying in droves due to suicide, so why am I so angry about the video? Maybe it's because expressing your feelings of pain and insecurity seems significantly easier to me than having to forget about your own feelings of pain and insecurity in order to single-handedly prevent the suicide of another person.

My reaction to the break-up was to take a break myself. I went home to Yorkshire. I deleted numbers, blocked social media accounts, and spoke to university professionals about DC's behaviour. I stuck to my guns. I put my foot down. I was very stoic in my understanding of what I was entitled to. This was a mistake in the end. I'd never have, although I probably should've, predicted the consequences.

Here is a comprehensive list of DC's demands over the course of our four-month relationship:

1) Love me unconditionally.

2) Devote your time to me.

3) Expect the proportion of devoted time to increase.

4) Do not complain.

5) Stop seeing your friends if it's time away from me.

6) Your house, bed, body, are all mine now.

7) Never leave.

8) Accept my suicidal threats as an understanding of what will happen if you do leave, and even though I'll apologise, know that those threats will always be there in the background

9) Allow me to plan your future against your will.

10) Your home is my escape now. It isn't yours.

11) If you fail me on any of these, even some I haven't mentioned, I will grow to be aggressive.

12) If you fail to love me after my aggression, I will attempt suicide, and I will be sure to let you know about it.

13) If you fail to forgive me still, I'll die.

I felt out of control and claustrophobic. I was desperately attempting to escape while guilt was clawing at me, refusing to let me leave, refusing to let me even live a normal life without it. Yet, to so many people it was DC who was the victim in our scenario, the one so desperately tortured and chained, the one who needed the protection, who it was my responsibility to save if only I'd tried a little bit harder. One day I hope to meet someone where their only expectation of me is that I don't kill myself if they leave. Such an easy thing to avoid. I could finally fulfil the expectations of others and my parents would be so proud.

I wonder where the viral videos are of people looking to help women like me. I'm glad we're finally discussing toxic masculinity and men's mental health issues. I'm happy about the new punk songs, the questions on political debate shows, and the adverts in train-stations asking men to check in on their "missing mates." But people only started caring when they realised toxic masculinity was hurting men. Women have been screaming for decades about how painful it is when men can't express their feelings in a healthy way. We experience emotional, sexual, and physical abuse as a consequence. It's hard, it hurts us, and we're suffering. The impact of young men with mental health issues isn't only dead men but dead women. Mentally ill men create mentally ill women. They bring us trauma; we scratch at yellow wallpaper. We get lobotomised, labelled as hysterical and unfit for leadership, and fifty years later, they are angry they can't cry as loudly as we do. Is it just me that feels no one is listening to our screaming? Perhaps our voices are too high, too shrill. Maybe only dogs can hear us.

This is bitter and self-centred. I'm projecting personal rage onto something much, much bigger. The issue of men's mental health absolutely should be brought to our attention, and it's right that we discuss male suicide. Still, I can't quiet the little voice inside the bitterest part of me that says, "They never seem to care about *our* dead bodies. Really, they don't care about us at all."

Or whatever, I don't know. The anger's there, but it is useless and I'm actively working to let it go. I don't have any answers. Maybe I just wish I were a better writer so that people would call me talented when I die.

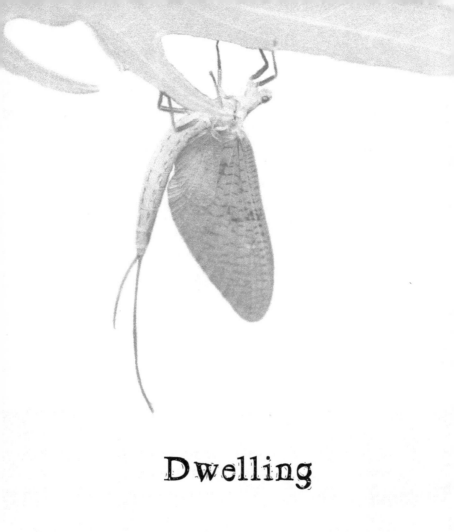

Dwelling

One day
I may kill myself
By way of
An apology.
One day
I may kill myself
To be
Like you
Again.

But not today, my darling,
Not today.

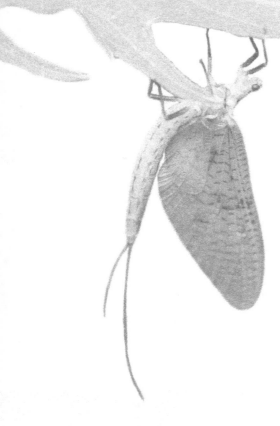

Funeral fantasies

Dreams tell me he's back and we're together and both of us are happy again. Whenever I wake up hungover, I waste the first few hours of my new day self-indulgently planning my funeral. I wonder who'll come. I wonder if they'll cry. I think about the songs that my loved ones will choose for me and whether anyone will wear black. In reality, I don't reach out to these people after fantasising about their devastation over my imaginary death. It's mortifying to speak to anyone about their feelings towards you. People find it uncomfortable, and it is uncomfortable.

We're constantly told that absence makes the heart grow fonder, so imagine the effect death has on it. The heart grows huge, bulging, painfully stretching the outside skin like an overly blown-up balloon. *(Metaphors again? Poor form. I should stick to the no-nonsense self-deprecation and stop trying so hard. Does a heart even have skin? What do we call an outer layer if not "skin"?)*

This is how I understand funerals to work. There's a lot of crying. If there's any luck, there's rain. There's a priest standing in front of everyone, probably offending a lot of atheists and comforting a lot of family members. If it's the funeral of Dan Collins, there will be some overt Catholicism which will seem both judgemental and inappropriate and yet totally and completely appropriate in a bitterly ironic way. People will drink and smoke too much and speak about him afterwards. The family will be kind, although they will want answers. Friends will speak about him and describe a character I'm unfamiliar with.

"He was a perfect, flawless, genius of a person, and I adored him so completely that now my heart is breaking."

This is the kind of thing we will all say to each other. I said many things like this at the funeral, with that exact level of intensity. There were also lots of anecdotes spilled. I was too drunk and socially unaware to consider the level of appropriateness of all of them, leading to many kind but awkward silences. But what would I have said to his face? I told him I loved him often, and I tried to build up his self-esteem as best I could when we were together, but after that, I just wanted him to leave me alone. The fact is, he often came across as arrogant. He seemed perfectly comfortable with his identity and the things he loved. It was only after digging further that we realised how unwell he truly was and how deeply the insecurities ran.

At the funeral, it was clear that people remembered him as a shy boy, someone quiet and unassuming, which blew us all away because he wasn't that person to us. He was DC. But he must have been that other DC too. We just hadn't met him.

Had he, in his last few moments, asked me: "Cathy, please explain your feelings towards me," I would have, beyond any shadow of a doubt answered: "My feelings are that I want you to leave me alone and stop stalking me, Dan Collins," which is if I'd have bothered to respond at all. Of course, that makes me buckle with guilt again, but realistically, what else could I have said?

I imagine the situation would be similar with my own funeral. My parents would be sad. Old friends would talk about me. But if I were to ask them now, "Mum, Dad, siblings, friends, how do you feel about me?" they would either ask me to stop bothering them or grab the opportunity to air some grievances. It may actually be useful. Harsh realities are something we all regularly need to stop us being terrible people.

I'm going to try and stop planning my own funeral now. I'll stop distantly planning a suicide I know I won't commit to. I don't think it helps anyone. It definitely doesn't help me. And regardless, I don't have the stomach for an overdose.

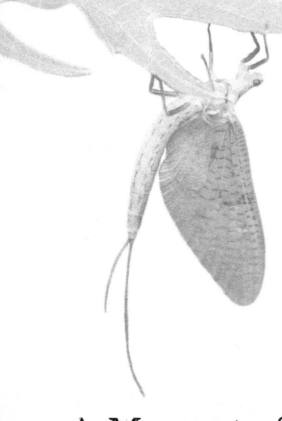

A Moment of Hope

Everyone loves a tragic story. I used to think that the presence of tragedy rounds something off with more maturity, seriousness, and intensity, but there is nothing mature about suicide.

Would Nirvana have been so iconic had Kurt Cobain not killed himself? I mean, maybe. They were very good. But we can't ever be certain. Cobain's entrance into the twenty-seven club and the tragedy surrounding the Nirvana story is partially what makes them so historically fascinating, at least it did for me when I was a grungy, teenage rat-bag. Don't all young people like to see themselves as tragic victims, angels too pure for our corrupt and violent world?

Sid Vicious died young and he murdered his girlfriend. He's a legendary punk icon. Johnny Rotten grew up, and now he advertises butter and is politically disappointing. They were both exploited seventeen-year-olds with problematic swastika armbands when they made it in the punk scene (arguably *made* the punk scene, although I still think The Buzzcocks are criminally underrated), but their legacies have gone in different directions and it's difficult to see why unless we account for tragedy. Tragedy makes history. Tragedy immortalises. Celebrities who recover from breakdowns often have those breakdowns held up as embarrassing signs of their weakness while celebrities who kill themselves after breakdowns have the breakdowns immortalised as iconic representations of their true talent. They were just too beautiful to live. Society is torture. In angst we trust, amen.

I'm guilty of glorifying mental illness and tragedy just as much as anyone else is. In fact, I may be guiltier than most. There's a reason all my short stories end in tragedy. It just adds more punch. It emphasises the grit and the brutality of this world in which we live. It shows I am deep and intellectual, I desperately hope, as I pen yet another story where sexual abuse and psychosis are indicated but never said aloud because ambiguity *also* signifies depth and intellectualism. Trust me, I have an MA in this nonsense. I know all the pretentious rules and follow them unironically while hating myself constantly.

This project differs from my other writing in that everything here is 100% true—or at least the truth from my perspective. I say this now because the following extract between my friend and I after Dan Collins' first suicide attempt is truly unbelievable. In fact, with suicidal families, stalking, psychotic breakdowns, ceremonial coincidences, and the portrayal of my ex-boyfriend as a vengeful ghost who is punishing me, this may be the least believable extract I have written so far.

I sat having tea with a good friend: a sweet, mothering, American friend who loves

English films and wanted to study abroad to embrace her Hugh Grant fantasy. She is kind, positive, and unpretentious. She likes romance novels and isn't ashamed of it. She knows very little about grunge.

"Imagine if he had died though," I said, still shaken and terrified from the night before (that line again, "We believe you are the cause" floating up in my memory). "I don't think I'd ever have recovered. Everyone would have blamed me."

"You can't say that! Even if it had happened, you absolutely shouldn't blame yourself," kind, motherly American friend said. "It would be like when Kurt Cobain died, if they…"

Oh no, I thought. Kind, American friend surely won't continue with this line of thought.

"… blamed it on his…"

Come on kind, American friend, you must know this is not a sensible road to go down.

"…daughter or something."

Quick recovery. Flawless really.

"But they very much did blame his wife, my kind, American friend. People were quite, quite angry with Courtney Love."

"Well, I know, I know, but still…"

Poor, kind American friend. She is a terrible chooser of analogies but a wonderful friend all the same.

The reason I bring Nirvana into this is because last night I had a moment of hope. In

Bilbao, there was a selection of cover bands playing American grunge and pop punk classics. There was fake Nirvana, fake Greenday, fake Foo Fighters, and fake Offspring—a Kerrang extravaganza of fakers. All good, clean, nostalgic fun. I was delighted. "Lithium" is never quite the same unless the words are muddled into Spanglish-spoken mumbles before an audience of drunken Basques scream out: "YEEEEEEAAAAAAAH!"

At some point, a woman came on stage to join fake Nirvana. They transformed, for three songs, into fake Hole. Musically speaking, it was quite awful. The girl was so stunningly beautiful though that I almost couldn't breathe watching her. Her hair exploded from her head in sandy, blonde waves, and she weighed perhaps all of four stone. She wore a leather boob-tube, leather trousers, leather boots, and she played a blue Fender guitar perfectly. Fake Courtney Love screamed into the microphone like she couldn't have cared less what people thought of her. She kissed the bassist. She danced. She did not sing in tune, but neither did Bob Dylan and I fell in love with him too for a brief period when I was seventeen. All the bands were fun but mediocre, as is correct and expected of cover bands. But Hole didn't make it onto the bill. She didn't get her own set. She was shoved into Nirvana's slot for three songs, and then she left, and fake Nirvana played "Smells like Teen Spirit" without her.

And I thought, fuck me, I really miss Hole. I hear Nirvana all the time. I have their records on vinyl. They're on my Spotify playlists and also the playlists of the clubs that I frequent. But Hole I rarely hear because they're not considered to be as good as Nirvana are. And people fucking hate Courtney Love. God, they hate her so much.

A brief note for Courtney Love

I don't think you did it, Courtney. I mean, it's quite apparent to everyone with common sense that you didn't, although I wasn't there and might be wrong. Still, I feel quite certain. I understand the pain of losing someone to suicide on a small-scale level, but under the eyes of adoring fans, I don't even know how you coped. Except I do because I know that coping isn't really a choice in the way that people think it is. Pain happens, and you can't opt out of it. Well, I suppose you can, but if that 'solution' is what put us all in this mess in the first place, you're much more likely to choose not to. Anyway, suicide is scary. The thought of razor blades across my wrists makes me cringe. I can't stand nausea, so pills would never work. I've never been that great at tying knots. Wanting to live isn't a sign of strength and bravery. I don't stay alive out of stubbornness. I do it out of a fear of nothingness. Still, we are here. And we are coping. Sort of. In a way. So, that's something.

I rode the metro home, and I listened to *Live Through This*. Nirvana might be better (in my humble and uneducated opinion), but Hole was still really good, too.

And I'm going to keep writing, Dan Collins. So, there.

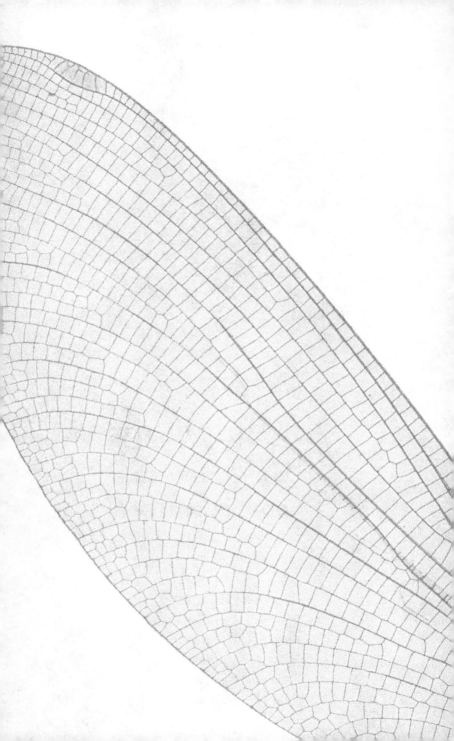

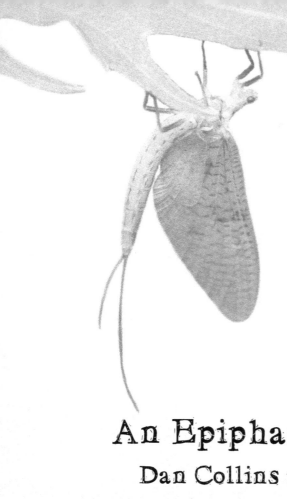

An Epiphany:

Dan Collins is
good, actually

On editing, I realise that I've not made the DC and Marvel universe particularly likable. In my representation of absolute reality, I've focussed on the horrendous truth that many would deny or prefer to ignore. I come across as self-absorbed, self-pitying, and pathetic, some moron pining over a pretentious idiot who tried too hard to be unconventional and creative during his brief existence. All of this is true. It's also not the whole truth. In worrying too much about whether or not I'm a writer, in focusing too much on his talent, I've left out all the most human details that made up DC. So here are some facts about Dan Collins the human, not Dan Collins the ghost, the genius, the demi-god, or the punisher. I'm realising that this will probably never be publishable. I still think it's important to get it all down.

1) We watched *Hell's Kitchen*. We also watched *RuPaul's Drag Race*, and I would tell him the history of all of the queens in *All Stars*, and he'd unironically ask me if this was my area of expertise. Effortlessly cool Sam Shepard plays and David Lynch films, this was not.

2) We cooked meals together before *Hell's Kitchen* and pretended that we hadn't used jarred sauce while Gordon Ramsey screamed at super-macho Americans for doing that exact thing. It was usually

pasta. I'm not the best cook. Sometimes he'd bring round a takeaway with wine, and that was always the most appreciated. I never understood how he had the patience not to eat his Subway on the bus.

3) For a Halloween party, he dressed up as a made-up superhero. He called himself "Captain Blackmail." I understand this now to be some kind of horrendous foreshadowing, but at the time, we thought it was hilarious. He wore a black eye-mask and spray painted a strip of his hair white. He sellotaped black envelopes and alphabetical letters over himself. The more you think about it, the more ridiculous the puns seem, and the more it seems to spill out into layers of absurdity. My favourite part was that the letters on the eye-mask very subtly wrote out "Fuck War."

4) Before we were together, DC spent hours convincing us that he had met a woman. This was during an online group chat while we all sat at home dejected and hungover. He described her as an old flame from the past. I think he called her Cherry. I was jealous. That was the first sting of realisation that I might have wanted to be more than friends. He gave an elaborate story about the night those

two had met before finally sending us a picture of himself in drag. I'm big enough to admit that I was very much a step-down from Cherry.

5) After the first night he stayed at my house, he sent me a survey asking me to explain a few things. He spoke about the way I'd levitated in my sleep. He asked me why I continued to let strange men enter my bed. I filled in the survey and sent it back, informing him that he'd misspelled vagina.

6) Before sex, he'd take off his jumper and t-shirt at the same time, then fling them across the room like he couldn't quite believe that it was going to happen. He could go from fully dressed to naked in less than eight seconds. I timed it once.

7) When I was discussing something presumably judgemental or pretentious in an attempt to impress our very cultured Mutual Friend of Great Importance, DC interrupted to say that he was going to get business cards printed that said "Bless You" so he could hand them out to those who sneezed in lectures. It took us a few seconds before we both burst out laughing. DC's face remained completely poker straight.

8) The next time that I saw him, he told me to meet him at the station for a "surprise." He wouldn't tell me what it was. In the end, when I got there, he revealed the "Bless You" cards. They were perfectly cut out and laminated, of course. DC, forever the perfectionist. Alongside the usual "Bless You" and "Excuse Me" cards, there were also some ridiculous ones: "I'm taking the kids," "I came," "God help us all." I wish I could remember the more hilarious sentences. We handed them out to anyone we could find, so I don't know where they all are now. I quite like that though. I like that they're around the world somewhere hidden in various wallets and in the bottom of handbags. I hope people keep handing them out without context.

9) Initially, I had him saved in my phone as "Weird Dan." Later that changed to Dan Collins. After a while it changed to "IloveyouDanCollins." This was before we'd so much as kissed. I used to shout it at him when I saw him on campus, walking with his legs kicking awkwardly side to side. (For some inexplicable reason, he always walked like a duckling). His response to my confessions of love were always a stiff: "Oh stop it, you red-headed whore."

10) For the first time in a long time, I read through our messages. He was naturally hilarious and quirky and all the rest of it, but with him, so was I. One thing I didn't remember is how naturally we interacted. I wasn't uncomfortable or awkward. I picked up and added to his jokes effortlessly, without any concern that I was getting it wrong. I'm not sure if I'll ever find anyone else who'll keep me so engaged. I miss who we were. We were good people. I've spent so long repressing that I loved him, instead choosing to express a well-versed defence of my actions. But I did love him. Very much so. For the most part, he was good.

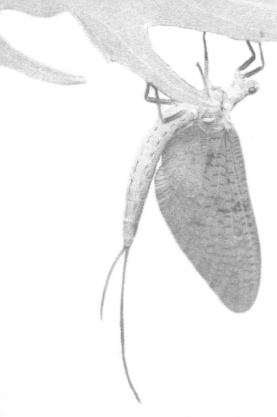

Delusional
Conversation #5:
A defence

Look at how well I'm doing, DC. Another story of mine got picked up by a magazine. I spoke to an old lecturer about it, and he seemed pleased to hear from me, and I think they call this networking, DC.

Look, I'm back on Tinder now and getting matches too. The other day a group of teenage boys spoke to me on the metro, and I think they must have fancied me because now they send me messages about meeting them in parks to drink cartons of cheap wine. I don't go. But all the same, watch me thriving.

Look at how many scenic places I'm visiting in Spain. Look at all these pictures of mountains and beaches. Isn't the sunset so beautiful, DC? Isn't it so marvellous that I'm still alive under all this sun? Look at my social media accounts. I'm getting likes and friend requests. I'm broadening my horizons and living my best life.

I sometimes think that I will stay here another year. Sometimes I think I'll finish my contract and leave. I'm reminded that I should just relax.

"Enjoy it," my co-workers say, handing me another drink. Look at me enjoying it. Look how much beer I drink now. Look how many cigarettes I smoke. Watch me relaxing. Watch me thrive.

I had sex yesterday, DC. Look at me: the single, empowered female. I was at a beautiful beach café with a very tall and handsome Spanish man, and he began to act quite awfully, DC. He said something despicable, and I decided to leave. Look at me stand up for my values. Look at the way I'm still swayed by intersectional feminism. Look at me.

On the metro home, I texted someone else to meet for a drink with every intention of having revenge sex, and I did. He spoke to me about his suicidal thoughts, and a part of me thought I should run, but a larger, more stubborn part told me to stay. Look at me, avoiding red flags out of spite.

He called himself a weirdo, and I said that I liked weirdos. At three in the morning, we were having sex in my apartment. I looked into his eyes while I lay underneath him, and it seemed like he wanted to hurt me. He liked to choke me, DC. Look at me pushing the boundaries of my sexuality. I asked him if he was going to kill me, and he smirked and didn't answer. It was a joke on his part, but I accepted my death quite easily. No one else knew who I was with that night. Look at my lack of foresight. Look at my spontaneity. Look at how well I'm doing.

Look at how many friends I have, look at how desperately I'm trying to move on, look at how privileged I am, look at how happy this song is, look at how logical I am, look how cultured, look how I put myself out there, look, DC, just look.

Don't you see how well I'm doing without you?

More Delusional Conversations.

The Anniversary Diaries

26.04.2019

I think what I'm feeling now is depression. This time last year, I was walking home from university. I'd stayed for a few drinks with friends after the first dissertation lecture. There was camp, screaming laughter, mimed sex-scenes, shocking confessions, and a very concerned Christian who didn't understand if we were joking or not. (I will forever love you kind, American friend.)

As I walked home, I listened to music and smoked a cigarette. I thought, *Thank god, DC didn't show*. It was the last time I was academically obliged to be in the same room as you. I'd agreed to meet good, kind, studious friends, while my rebellious bar-friends agreed to meet you. I was going to arrive early and leave early. Rebellious bar-friends would prevent you from following me home by dragging you to the bar again. I had the number for campus security saved on my phone just in case.

But you didn't show. Rebellious bar-friends arrived at the lecture ten minutes late and without you in tow. Mutual Friend of Great Importance made a joke: "Sorry for our lateness, lecturers. It was entirely the fault of this one particular, rebellious bar-friend," and the room snickered and they sat down. He shrugged at me to let me know that he didn't know where you were. *Thank God.*

So, I got to stay for drinks afterwards instead because I didn't have to run away from you. We all agreed that it was for the best you hadn't shown. I remember saying that I sometimes missed you, and it was such a shame how all of this had panned out because I couldn't really have good conversations with others in the same way that I could with you. Not that I would ever consider getting back with you. That ship had obviously long sailed. My friends agreed with me that yes, it was a shame.

So, we drank our drinks, we smoked our fags, and we made our lewd jokes, and I walked home with a slight weight off my shoulders because you hadn't shown. Thank God.

The next morning I'd get a phone-call from Mutual Friend of Great Importance. You told your mother ("Mother") that you were leaving for the seminar, but you hadn't come home. She'd just wanted to check with our Mutual Friend of Great Importance that you were still safely at his house because she'd assumed you'd stayed over. But you'd never gone to the seminar, had you? You definitely weren't at his house.

That phone call was followed by many from the police, each with the exact same tone they'd had during the first attempt ("We believe that you're the cause...") and I felt ill, with worry yes, but mostly with anger because I was sick of you constantly pulling these stunts.

It wasn't a stunt though, was it DC?

Yesterday, I went to the beach. It was nice. I went to a popular tourist spot with some friends, and we climbed up some ruins and took in the scenery. At the top of San Juan de Gaztulegatxe, there's a small church. There's a bell that people ring three times while their parents, partners, or friends take pictures. After ringing the bell, they make a wish. Inside the church, there's a small stand which sells cold drinks and souvenirs. Nautical paintings and stained-glass windows decorate the walls.

The place is very popular for tourists because in *Game of Thrones,* Jon Snow stares broodingly from the top of it for a few seconds. I tried to pray for you in this bullshit, consumerist setting. I bought a shitty candle for one euro fifty and I lit it from one of the others at the front of the church. I assumed it was Catholic. Most churches here are Catholic. I don't know if that would really matter to you. I asked you to please look after me, to please forgive me for trying to move on. I searched myself internally to see if I actually believed this was working, if any of my self-hatred was being released. There's a big difference between the girl in 2018 smoking her cigarette and walking home in the dark, grateful to be rid of her stalker—the atheist, the feminist, the rational thinker who tried her best to be compassionate, but not if it compromised her safety in any way—and the girl in 2019 near tears in front of a tourist spot, trying desperately to believe in something because she isn't sure what she thinks anymore.

Tourists everywhere continue to ring the bell three times and ask for cans of Coke in loud American accents.

My friends asked if I was religious.

"No," I said. "It's just nice to do things like that sometimes."

These people don't know that you're dead, DC. They don't know that you ever existed. I wonder if they've ever noticed me look solemn.

I've been to some new beaches. I've looked at some cool buildings. I would trade all those memories to be back on that walk home on the 26th of April 2018, smoking my cigarette, listening to music, and feeling grateful that my stalker hadn't shown. I don't think tragedy causes personal growth, DC. I think it makes you question everything about yourself. I think I'm now so uncertain of who I am and what happened that I'm no longer a complete person, and this doesn't make me deep. It doesn't make me thin, dark, and tortured. I'm not Jon Snow brooding at the top of a mountain. I'm just as spotty; my hair is just as thin. I'm just as socially awkward, just as much of an oversensitive over-sharer (evidently). This experience has not made me a better writer. It's not made me more intense or secretive or fascinating. It's just me, except with more pain. But yeah, I've seen some new beaches. So, I guess that's something.

27.04.2019

Did you die on this date? Was it today? We know exactly when you disappeared and we know when the body was found, but two full days seems a long time for an overdose. It's a long time to be in pain, dying, and waiting to be discovered. What else happened? What did you do? Did you walk away from the house, post the letter, and then go down the road where you used to walk your dog, and take the overdose? Was it that quick, that simple?

I wonder if you walked by the canals and thought about where you were from and the memories you had there. I wonder if you stopped by my house. I wonder if you sat at a bus stop first, thinking about whether you should go to the dissertation meeting, whether you should forget all your kamikaze plans. Did you try to call me and realise the number was still blocked? What else did you do, Dan Collins?

Today, I read the presentation you left for me. It made me cry, but I was happy. I'd avoided our conversations for so long because they were too painful, but today I needed pictures of you, and I found them. You were so sweet about me. I think you must have loved me really. Then again, were you just grovelling because you had an ulterior motive, and you thought admitting all wrong was the best way to get me back? I have so many questions and no answers. I'll never get answers now.

When you first died, I had nightmares about you coming back. I used to imagine it in a public space, a crowded living room with everyone who I'd briefly met at the funeral, and while they all hugged you and cried and were elated to see you, you'd look to the door for me. I'd walk in last, and everyone would stare at me, *and marvel*. I'd scream, cry, and beat you back. Once, when having this dream, I woke up screaming, "Don't touch me!" It started as a horrible fantasy and then it reoccurred in my subconscious. I used to wake up scared and hysterical, horrified at the thought of having to see you again because I was too angry with you to cope. I'd comfort myself through the tears by remembering that you weren't coming back. Nihilism was a comfort then.

I'm not really angry anymore, but I am very, very sad. I want to run to your gravestone and say, "I get it now. I'm over it. Just come back, and we won't speak about it again." Death is such a permanent thing and emotions are so fleeting. What a waste, my love. What an awful, awful waste.

I would kill for that room now. I'd kill to see you comfortable, surrounded by the people you love. I'd walk in last, and proudly, and I'd hug you in front of everyone knowing that there was nothing to be scared of and no reason for shame. We'd start again. This could be a blip in an otherwise happy existence. But it won't happen, I know, and the fantasies have long stopped being comforting. I think at one point I made you happy. I really hope I did.

Many, many moons ago, when things were normal and good between us, we were at a party with our Mutual Friends. Another couple—a very happy, normal couple—spoke to us. They were having a disagreement (one of those endearing, disingenuous ones) about what song would be "their song." They had different ideas, not least because one of them was Mutual Friend of Great Importance, and he was of all things musically conventional. You both detested unoriginality. His partner asked us:

"Do you two have a song?"

And you'd replied:

"We have albums."

We began to list all the records we played while we drank together, all the bands we'd argued about in depth. (What is the best David Bowie album of all time? Will anyone ever know this for certain either?) Today, I made a playlist with all those albums. I'll listen to all of it until the songs are done. I hope this is enough to show I care. But who am I showing my care to? Is there any point in sentimental gestures for the dead?

28.04.2019

This is the day, DC. I woke up hungover, and I think it's only appropriate that I feel as sleep-deprived and nauseous as I did this time last year. I wonder if this is self-indulgence or self-flagellation. Mutual Friends are getting in touch to see if I'm okay, and I can't tell if they really want to hear from me or if they're asking out of some sense of duty in the same way you go to the funerals of the relatives you couldn't really stand. I don't know what I'm supposed to do for you today. I made the playlist already. I looked through all the photos. I want to watch your favourite film, but I really don't want to watch your favourite film. I want to cry, but I would love to get through the day without crying.

I tried to go to some churches, but they were closed. Surprising for a Sunday. I don't know if it would've brought me any comfort anyway. I don't really believe in anything religious, but I associate Catholicism so much with you. Perhaps it's all true. Maybe there's a part of you still out there watching over me. I don't think so, but who's to say it isn't true? I'm becoming more agnostic by the day, although it doesn't matter anyway because the churches are all closed.

This main issue is that I'm self-centred, which is about the worst thing anyone can be. Before you died, I used to listen to a song and maybe I'd like it. Now, I listen to a song and like the song and feel cripplingly depressed that I didn't write the song myself, that I don't know the people who wrote the song personally, that I'm not part of the genre's subculture, and life is fading away from me day-by-day with an overwhelming quickness, and I don't think I'll ever be happy with where I am or what I've accomplished. As a result, I can't enjoy the song, although I like the song, and the whole thing leaves me feeling ashamed of who I am. But the song isn't a reflection of me. Not everything is about me. It's just a fucking song.

To an extent, I understand why you did this, DC. It's horrible to not like who you are. It's difficult to see life happening in front of you while unable to live it to its full potential. I wish there was someone else controlling all my actions, driving me towards the things that might make me happy. But no, I am completely responsible for myself, and I go through life so tentatively, failing completely to build up any kind of dignity. Because life is so precious and so easy to lose and every day it's slipping away, and I'm shortening my lifespan with the stress of not knowing how to prevent my time here from being a complete waste. Even this rambling is self-centred. I should be focusing on you, but the churches are closed, and I don't know what else to focus on.

I read a book once when I was younger. It was the kind of book you wouldn't have liked. It was accessible and written to be enjoyed by a large, uneducated audience. There was a woman whose husband had died in a car-crash, and she suffered tremendously from the loss. The book ended a year after the accident. The character looked out of the window and saw a butterfly, and this helped her to feel some sense of acceptance. She finally felt happy and allowed herself to move on to a new relationship with someone who'd been waiting on the side-lines throughout the novel. I remember reading this as a child and thinking that a year seemed like an awfully long time to be miserable.

When we met your mother ("Mother"), she gave us some things to remember you by, the things that you'd left us in the will. This is where I got the books that have since been stolen or accidentally given away, and the David Bowie records we never agreed on. A white butterfly landed on the pub table where we were all drinking and smoking, and your mother ("Mother") pointed to it and said whenever she saw white butterflies, she thought it was you watching over us.

It's been a year now, and I can't see any butterflies. I don't think I'll ever get to the stage of accepting that this has happened. At no point in my life will this stop being a sad event. I think I should stop writing here. This piece doesn't have any point or any sense of resolution. And how can I find resolution when the churches are all closed?

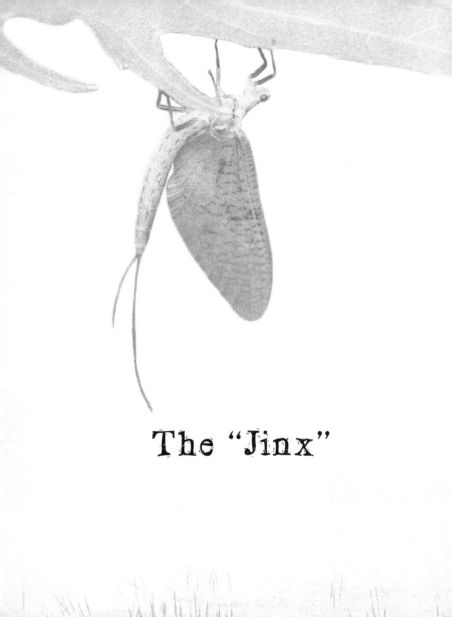

The "Jinx"

I don't watch football because I'm not the biggest fan of sport, but in that summer after DC's death, I used every opportunity handed me to leave the house. Someone invited the group round to watch the semi-final of the World Cup. I missed the first half, but I got there for the second.

I remember when I was little, and my family would watch sport. My dad's a soft, kind man, but he shouts at the top of his voice if the players don't do what he'd like them to. My mum's the same with rugby. I can't stand the sound of people screaming. It's loud and makes me panic. In my dream world, everyone would speak in low, clear voices while wearing soft fabric and hanging up jingling wind-chimes. When I was little, my family were crammed into the living room watching a World Cup or something. The two sofas faced each other, and the television was mounted on the perpendicular wall, meaning people had to lie down to really watch it. This took up a lot of space, and there wasn't often room enough for everyone. I was bored. Normally, I was left alone to watch TV, but now the TV was being used, and I needed someone to play with. I wasn't allowed in the room when the football was on. I asked questions about the match, and people got annoyed because I didn't understand. I was distracting. This game was *important*, so I couldn't come in.

But when you're little, two hours can seem like days, and I had no distractions and nothing to do (or I probably did, but at the time it didn't feel like it). At one point, I walked into the room and both my parents and my brother screamed at me to go away. It was before I'd started speaking—as soon as they'd seen my face peep round the door. I remember my brother particularly because he told me to fuck off, and no one shouted at him for swearing. I ran up to my room and cried. I cried for what felt like a long time. Eventually, I stopped because I realised no matter how loud and dramatic I deliberately made it, no one was going to come and check on me. Our team lost, and everyone was irritated.

The few times my family watched sport after that, it felt like the team we liked always lost. This could be a distorted memory, again, a possible result of my need to cling onto everything negative. I convinced myself that I was a jinx and that I shouldn't watch the games because my being there would ruin it for everyone. As a grown-up, I realised this was nonsense. That's why I was happy to watch with my friends, who were able to talk about the football while watching the football without anyone telling them to shush. No one shouted. We drank beer. This was a social event. Even though people cared, and there was clearly a high-strung atmosphere, no one took that out on the guests, particularly not the vulnerable, alcoholic messes whose boyfriends had just died. But when I turned up, England started to lose. I missed the first half and got there just in time for the second, then it all went to pot. It was only forty-five minutes and everything in British summer went from positive to negative, and I realised I'd ruined the whole "it's coming home" vibe for an entire country.

A few beers later, standing outside the flat smoking cigarettes and talking about the football, I told my friends my theory. I said they'd only started losing when I started watching. My friend's boyfriend said:

"Jesus, you mean to say that you've not seen England score a single goal this entire season?" and I attempted to tell them that it was precisely *because* I hadn't seen it that they *had* scored so many goals this season, that my watching had been the cause of the distinctive lack of goals in the second half of their final game. Another friend asked me:

"Are you seriously holding yourself accountable because we didn't do well in a fucking football match?"

And I had to explain that, no, not really, I knew it was nonsense because I'm a very mature, adult cynic who dabbles in nihilism, has zero qualms about their atheism and couldn't possibly believe in such ridiculous things as superstition or jinxes, but that yes I did to some extent believe that my watching the football game is what caused England to drop out of the World Cup. It's absurd, and insanely narcissistic, but there's still a part of me scared to write it down in case people see the truth and grow angry at me. *(Reader, are you angry? I promise that if it was my fault, it really wasn't intended. Maybe my writing would do well with a Croatian audience.)*

I planned to end this section with a joke about how, despite not truly believing it, I'd still vow never to watch a World Cup match again. Actually, I'm not going to do that. Instead, I'm going to think rationally, and I'm going to be positive for a change. I look forward to 2022. I don't know what exactly we'll be doing as a country or how far we'll get in the competition. To be honest, I don't understand leagues, rules, or qualifiers. Four years is a long way away, and I'm not sure what country I'll be in or what I'll be doing. I might not be alive, what with my horrendous lifestyle, my unhealthy stress-levels, and my propensity to undertake basic tasks carelessly (like crossing the road or deciding whether or not to drink cyanide). But one thing I'll be certain to do is to watch the World Cup. If I have friends, I'll invite them round. I'll get in beers and crisps. I'll encourage people to speak about their day while the match is on in the background, but I'll keep my eyes rooted to the screen. I'll watch if they score goals, and I'll watch when they lose, and I'll join in with any melody the crowd are chanting, but I'll sing my own words: "None of this has anything to do with me. None of this has anything to do with me. None of this has anything to do with me."

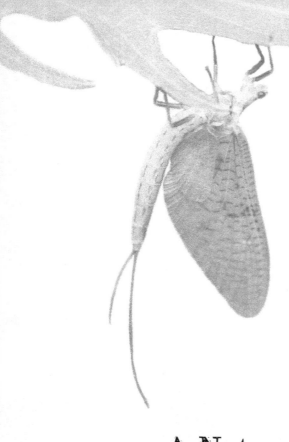

A Note of
(Unsolicited) Advice

I sleep so badly I often force myself awake halfway through reoccurring dreams out of sheer boredom. I eat so poorly that I feel weight-gain before the scales do. I'm falling so quickly that I'm beginning to look forward to the landing because then I can at least take stock of this situation, despite the broken bones, and I can begin to piece together what happened prior to the fall. You don't realise how much you're suffering until your body starts to betray you. It's something I have to use as an indicator of my general wellbeing. I might *feel* upset, but I'm clearly not *actually* hurt until I get insomnia, bald-spots, and an eye infection. Anything less than that is temporary sentimentality which too shall pass.

At the time of DC's death, I felt guilty because I wasn't sad enough. Aside from a week-long sabbatical in Yorkshire spent in drunkenness and complete denial, the weeks and months after DC's death, I was mostly fine. I functioned. I got up, I practiced Duolingo, and I did some exercise. I learned some basic Spanish verbs. I got better at yoga. I went to all my dissertation meetings, often with enthusiasm, and I continued to go out and drink with my friends. We drank an astounding amount that summer because it was very hot, and because we were doing well in the World Cup, and because despite all this, we were incredibly depressed. I showered every day, and I carried on going to work. All was well and good.

Except of course it wasn't because the wellness was completely destroyed by my sense that *nothing* should be well and good, and that I was awful for attempting to experience life so healthily. My stubborn insistence on feeling pain, and my perplexity at the lack of it, was never explained. But I was in pain. I must have been. I know this because my teeth hurt.

To anyone who's suffering and who may wish to read what some self-important idiot has to say, I want to let you know that you can never grieve too little. There may be microscopes pointing down on you but pay them no mind if you can help it. I trust there isn't anyone refusing to be genuinely miserable enough after death, and anyway, in terms of insincerity, I much prefer those who pretend to be unaffected than those who pretend to be devastated. Being too happy is an impossible feat and no one is ever suffering too little.

This comes to my mind because my friend has a toothache. She told us about it in perfect English while translating some words into Spanish. I was the only English person in the group and the rest couldn't speak as well as she could, so translation was a requirement. It was very kind. I still feel like a burden when people speak English for my sake alone, and yet isolated when people speak Spanish and

I struggle to follow. She was frustrated with the school who insinuated she only had the toothache because of stress.

"Qué no," she explained, "it's not because of stress. I sleep well. I have days off work where all I do is sleep and watch TV, and yet I still suffer from the toothache. I think I need some root-canal work."

"It seems to be oddly dismissive to me," I intervened, "because toothache is rarely caused by stress. Perhaps if you were losing weight or hair, but teeth?"

"I think," someone else explained to me, "that when you get stressed, you clench your jaw tight, and that makes your teeth hurt. Particularly in your sleep."

"Oh yeah, of course," I said.

I didn't say that I remembered this clearly from the way MDMA made average-looking people appear so chiselled in all of their Facebook photos. It took two days before I could eat when I experimented with drugs, and it was evidently never worth it. I find my speech embarrassing enough without the slurring. I couldn't handle the difficulty of a bruised and damaged jaw, and my memory from that night has disappeared forever into some void. I was left with jaw ache and a vague sense that I might have felt happy.

When Dan Collins died, I couldn't move my mouth correctly, and there was a constant ache in the bone under my ear. I never usually ground my teeth in my sleep, but I began to. Then I began to grind my teeth when I was awake. There was this sensation of helplessness as I felt my body clench, tense, and react in ways I wasn't telling it to. This caused issues with my diet.

I tried to eat when he was missing and regretted it when angry family members knocked on my door to question me about his disappearance. When they saw the delivery boxes, it gave the impression that, of course, I was totally fine, continuing with my life, stuffing my face while they were so worried sick and unable to concentrate on anything but the safe return of their son. I remember this with shame as I remember a lot of moments from my life with shame. I was eating greasy food, and they were already grieving.

While I was hibernating in the family home after the body was found, I tried to eat as normal. It reassured my parents when they saw me eating something, and anyway, it helped to break up the monotony of grief. When days are split into depressing phone calls and sporadic naps, it's good to cling onto some sense of time, and meals offer that. I felt guilty about eating because I should have been more upset, and anyway Dan Collins would never get to eat again. I forced myself to and then hated myself for not only managing to do it but actively enjoying the tastes. I remember at the time thinking that this is exactly why I would always be too cowardly to kill myself because even if my life was in utter shambles, I would still crave the taste of food, the smell of coffee, the satisfaction of cigarettes. I had to remind myself that *joie de vivre* is not cowardly. But I couldn't eat as much as I normally did, no matter how much I tried to, because there was always this pain in my jaw that wouldn't subside. I almost didn't notice it, or else I must have numbly accepted it, but my teeth were constantly sensitive because I was grinding them so much. I wonder if others noticed while I remained oblivious to it. It's rare for me to experience something new and painful and to refuse to analyse the source.

Recently, a loved one told me that they were glad I was enjoying life now. Yes, I was still burying myself away, avoiding normal social interaction, and feeling cripplingly self-conscious whenever I engaged in any conversation, but they felt that I was doing better than before.

"What was wrong with how I was doing before?" I asked, forever one to take the negative away from the positive and dig into exactly how I'm flawed.

Nothing was wrong with me, the person responded, but there was a greyness surrounding me that didn't ever seem to evaporate. I wasn't enjoying things like I used to, and they could tell. They were glad to see me enjoying myself again.

This was news to me. I'd assumed I was enjoying things just as much as usual and indeed felt sickened at myself because of that. It goes to show that pain doesn't always mutate and deform faces. It doesn't always scream and insist on being felt. The burns you have to worry about the most are the ones you can't feel because they indicate nerve damage.

I wish someone had a video recording of my life so that I could witness all my memories while sitting comfortably. I'd be content to re-experience the tough parts in order to gain a clearer perspective on whether my feelings are justified. I have this tendency to make connections, often tenuous ones which don't necessarily represent the truth. I'm convinced of the truth of Dan Collins because in that instance I was the sane one, but anything with links to childhood or trauma (and what is childhood, really, but many years of learned trauma that build into a personality?) I don't trust. I think I was an unhappy child. I'm told I was cheerful and lively. I thought I was coping brilliantly. The long-lost memory of an aching jaw tells me otherwise.

I urge anyone who feels they aren't suffering hard enough to check the body. Check the teeth, check the sleeping pattern, consider why your sore throat is making everything so difficult to swallow, consider why you've had a sore throat for so many weeks, and swallow anyway. Eat well. Drink herbal teas. Do yoga. It won't fix a thing, but it also won't hurt, and if you can't convince those around you, the least you can do is attempt to convince yourself. Trust you are depressed enough. Does this bring you comfort? Does this eradicate the guilt you'll inevitably feel anyway? Ah, well, eat your vegetables. Do some fucking yoga.

New "Love"

I call this "New Love," but it isn't. It's new comfort, new crush, new wondering if they're going to text back—all very cutesy and cringe-inducing. This lad I fancy isn't someone who has understood and responded to the deeper pain inside of me. He hasn't wiped my tears away with gentle, calloused hands, nor have I expressed my anguish to him or explained the inner workings of my trauma-ridden soul. We've not connected. I'm twenty-three and slightly chubby and I drink too much when I'm nervous and then snog boys on the beach. Not love. New silliness. But new something, all the same.

And what's real, authentic love supposed to be anyway? They tell me those couples who've been together a matter of months don't understand real love, that real love is the kind that grows over years. In my experience, my feelings are most intense at the beginning of a relationship when it's new and exciting, then again at the end when you're aware it's all going to go away, but supposedly it's this sweet spot in the middle that indicates the true intensity of genuine feeling. I'm not sure I believe in romantic love as a separate entity in and of itself. Perhaps it's just the same love and affection you feel with family and friends, but with the unhealthy addition of lust and ownership. Asexual and polyamorous people may disagree with this. Many counsellors have told me that my view of love is warped, regardless.

The fact I can't control how others feel about me is horrifying. I don't know if the person I've chosen to love might just drop me one day. I have this tremendous fear of abandonment and get desperately concerned that I, as a person, am simply awful and only getting worse, fundamentally evil and unlovable and undeserving of affection in the first place.

How does anyone deal with new relationships? What if you do the wrong thing without realising? What if they completely lose interest? What if they fall in love with someone else? All of this is entirely feasible.

Panic grips me. Suddenly, I'm realising I have to make choices in everything; how to behave, how to act, what to say, when to kiss, when to touch, whether to make the joke, whether to be quiet, to drink or not to drink, to move forward aiming to maintain the affection, or to abandon it altogether through fear of feeling the inevitable hurt. All of this is on my mind constantly, turning me into a frozen, panicked block of wood, lying between the bedsheets of a sad boy's bedroom, realising that yes, I have some control over the future, but no, I have no idea how my actions will affect the outcome. Perhaps this boy will only love me if my breath is always minty fresh. Perhaps I need to find a better way to handle hair removal. Maybe I shouldn't spend so much time writing ridiculous stories. Maybe I should try very hard to be less self-involved. But this, all along, is what I wanted. This is what I promised myself I'd wait for.

When Dan Collins died, I made a deal with myself. Dan Collins was a nice boy and I liked him. I didn't get palpitations when I saw him across a crowded room; I wasn't immediately struck with lust the second I met him. He was a friend, I grew fond of him, he adored me, and we got close. *Then* I fell in love with him after months of build-up, *then* the yearning and the heartache happened. I'd listen to one of his anecdotes and realise I was enamoured by him. I'd lean out my bedroom window shouting at him to come up, and he would smile at me like he loved me, and I'd feel my heart burst. It grew with time.

This meant that I had a healthy outlook on my worth throughout the relationship. I'd been so confident with him. I knew that he found me attractive. I could see he was somewhat in awe of me. It was his first real relationship, and it's very easy to confuse the feelings of comfort and happiness garnered from *any* relationship as a special affection for that one particular person. In a first relationship, you're not aware of reoccurring patterns. I gave him sex and love and emotional comfort, so therefore I must have been the best person in the world, except that I wasn't, and there were millions of women out there who could have offered him that same thing. But I embraced it. I allowed myself to feel confident. I slept in my teeth-retainer. I didn't always have time to shave my legs. I spoke honestly about my feelings, even the ones that were irrational or didn't seem particularly kind, because I felt it was important that he knew who I was and how I felt, even if it didn't reflect well on me as this perfect, angelic figure. I didn't have that same insecurity which usually follows me whenever I'm involved in some intense, tiresome, unreciprocated crush.

When that affection faded and I left, I had no qualms about staying away from him. I wanted to stay away from him. It wasn't just the stalking and the anger and the abusive behaviour; it was the smaller things too—details that shouldn't have mattered but did. I thought there might be better options out there for me. I thought that he was only just my age, and perhaps that was too young and immature. I realised that I sometimes found his comments annoying and pretentious, and I felt this obscure character he'd invented was disingenuous. I got irritated when he disrupted lectures with inane, dead-pan comments, and when he pandered to everyone around him, blindly agreeing with what they said. I was beginning to get frustrated by his insincerity. I thought perhaps I wanted someone who could give me heart palpitations when they looked at me from across the room.

Poor Dan Collins. He'd built up my self-esteem so much I really started to believe I was loveable

DC died in a grand, romantic gesture, one I'd never asked for, one I was resentful of and sickened by. By the time he went missing, I believed myself to be emotionally checked out. I was angry, I was scared, I was frustrated that he was attempting to ruin my life, and I regretted ever giving him the time of day. Then the body was found. The confident girl who knew her worth was suddenly this cold-hearted bitch who broke the heart of the boy who loved her, the only boy who'd ever love her this much. That confident girl who did this should never have existed. Dan Collins was the reason she came out, and with his death, she too must die. DC died because I hadn't leaned into the relationship entirely. I was having fun, but I didn't want the two of us to last forever. I knew I wanted to travel, and I wouldn't be getting married at twenty-two.

I'd had boyfriends much more abusive than DC, and I stayed around much longer. I'd been so smitten, so unreservedly dependent on them that it was up to them to leave. None of them had died. Those times it was only me who'd gotten hurt. I promised myself that what happened with DC wouldn't happen again because I'd stop it. I would never be with anyone I wouldn't dedicate my life to, never touch anyone who didn't give me heart palpitations from across the room. From the death of Dan Collins onward, I would only love when I knew I had every intention of staying, no matter how awful they were, no matter how much it hurt. I could never risk leaving anybody again, so the relationship I next got into would have to be intoxicating. It was unlikely. It was unrealistic. It would never happen like that, and if it did, it would be years down the line when I was ready to settle and commit.

But now there's some bell-end on the beach with a shitty hand tattoo, and he's giving me heart palpitations.

I'm sure in some patriarchal, red-pill part of the internet, someone could explain to me about punching up and punching down. They'd give everyone in this scenario a numerical value or something equally dehumanising, but I don't think feelings are as simple as that. It's more often to do with the situation you're in, the circumstances of meeting, and a variety of other, boring, unromantic but practical factors that indicate how deeply you fall. I don't think people should get what they ask for because now I'm getting heart palpitations. I'm terrified and guilty and messy and just as depressed as I was when I cried over DC's pictures and read through old messages.

But there's a spark of something that's potentially hope. Not hope because of the Boy on the Beach. No, there are millions of people out there who'd give me heart palpitations, but hope that this isn't the end of love as I know it. Maybe at some point, I can be alright.

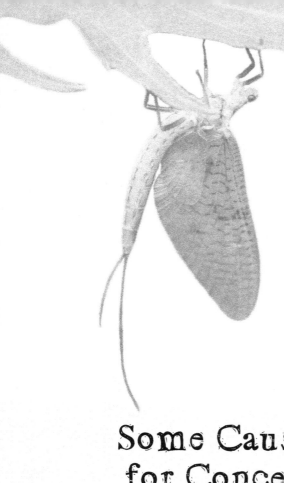

Some Causes
for Concern

The Boy on the Beach knows he's good-looking. He knows he's good with women, and as much as he swears blind that he's really a sensitive boy, the truth of his wide-spread ability to cause palpitations soon became known. The Boy on the Beach loves women, but not confident women, not women who feel too good about themselves, because he regards that as arrogance. The Boy on the Beach told me he should have known not to trust his ex-girlfriend when he told her she was beautiful, and she responded with: "I know." And yet, The Boy on the Beach sends me topless pictures of his chiselled abs and zero percent body fat with little to no prompting on my part. The Boy on the Beach told me, as we lay between crumpled bedsheets on my single bed that "You don't know what kind of effect you have on me," and just as I started to look at myself and think that perhaps I wasn't a hideous, fat, train-wreck of a mad person, he added, "But I think that's what I like most about you—you don't know," so I abandoned the thought to appease him.

The Boy on the Beach would explain to me that he didn't want a relationship. He would say that as much as he liked me (and he did, he assured me with a practiced sincerity, like me) he preferred spending time with his friends, and he couldn't give me everything I wanted. When he hadn't met with me as planned, I'd gotten upset and seemed clingy, and honestly, that set off alarm bells for him. I thanked him for his honesty. I understood there was nothing intrinsically immoral about wanting a laid-back relationship. It had been a nice month, and I was ready to leave. It was sad. My ego was bruised. The palpitations would become a distant shadow from the past, but I would recover.

But no, he said. There was no reason for this to be over. The Boy on the Beach, who was now on a quiet mountainside, explained to me that he did still like me (again this practiced sincerity), and perhaps we could see how this would develop, but slowly, without commitment, just for a little while.

Any self-respecting woman would know the correct thing to do is to leave. No one would agree to this haphazard nonsense knowing that it'll lead to unanswered texts and the further development of feelings that have already proven to be pointless. A self-respecting woman would refuse to be used as a sex-toy for a boy who doesn't appreciate their inner strength and beauty.

If we have learned anything thus far, it's that I'm not a self-respecting woman. I nodded and agreed to go along with Boy on the Beach to see how it played out.

I knew entering into this I'd get my heart broken, but when that happened, I wouldn't kill myself. I imagined it would be strangely liberating.

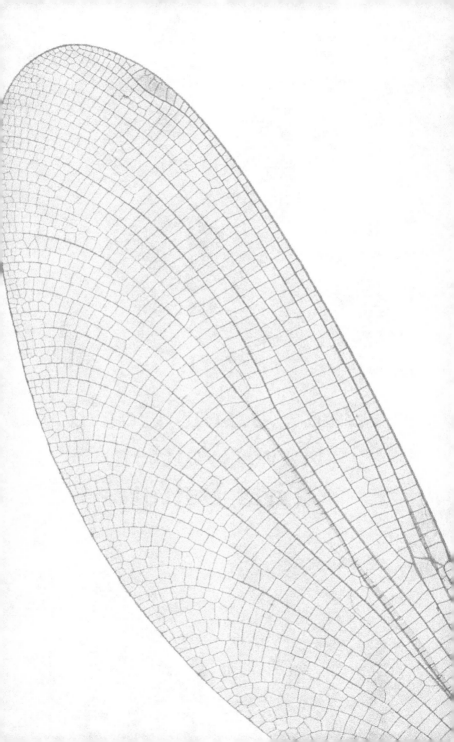

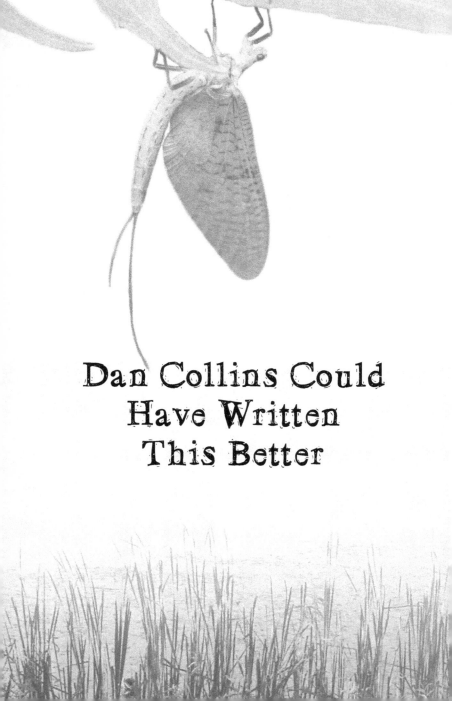

Dan Collins Could
Have Written
This Better

(A Villanelle)
We lie alone together, and we drink
Unspoken, we are touching skin to skin,
All these sensations make it hard to think.

You carry your black notebook
stained with ink
Show me stigmata nightmares
weaved from sin
We lie alone together and we drink

When you kissed me, I felt my
stomach sink
In darkness, heard your lips stretch
to a grin.
All these sensations make it hard to think.

We're laughing now, our faces
flushing pink
Hearing the record's empty static spin,
We lie alone together and we drink.

I wonder now what pushed you to
the brink.
I try hard not to let the answers in.
All these sensations make it hard to think.

We pass around the bottles with a clink
Your loved ones left to take it on the chin
We lie alone together and we drink.
All these sensations make it hard to think.

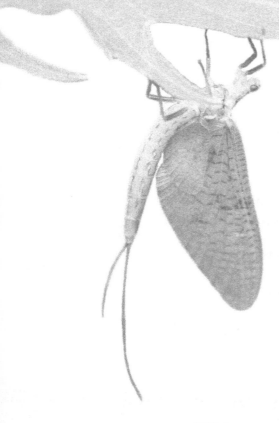

The
Ceremony Theory

Art will drive you insane. You'll stare at the same word for so long, you'll no longer be sure if it really is a word. You'll look at the same image repeatedly until you decide that slashing it with a scalpel is the only way to give it any meaning. You convince yourself that, in order to finish a creative writing dissertation, you need to spend forty minutes colouring in a tampon with brown lipstick. A repeated word will seem fine in one sentence but ridiculous over the course of a novel. Everything is brought into question until you reach a stage of dada-like absurdity, and you can't do anything but dwell on the meaninglessness of trying to make art because anyway, what is "good" art, what is "bad" art, what is "talent"? How do we define anything in this huge mass of meaninglessness? As a result, you send off stories to be rejected and graded poorly because you're stuck in this creative insanity, convinced that all art is valid, and everything is genius. But everything isn't genius, and all that happens is you put the art away and come back six months later, and suddenly it's so obviously apparent where the flaws lie and where the potential might be that you feel blind for never having seen it before.

I think, to a small extent, I've done this with Dan Collins, and I haven't seen the forest for the trees. I meticulously analysed every word he said, attempting to extract as much meaning as possible from this whole pointless and tragic ordeal, doing anything I could to force things to make sense. I don't know if this has been helpful, harmful, or if it's neither particularly, but instead a natural part of grief. I'm neurotic at the best of times, so it was obvious I'd react like this, worrying obsessively about everything that could have been done to prevent his suicide, analysing my own behaviour to find the exact moment I caused things to go wrong. I wanted to feel his thought patterns, to know exactly how he was feeling and what his motives were. Was it simply an act of revenge and bitterness? Did he really want to die? Did he know he was going to kill himself before he even met me? I became obsessed with "Ceremony."

Ian Curtis died at twenty-three. He had one more year than Dan Collins got at least. I went through stages of being unable to listen to any music that sounded good because goodness felt like pain. In the months that followed DC's death, I listened to a lot of industrial, noise, metal, electronic, punk, gibberish etc. Large walls of sounds coming at me so hard I couldn't be in pain because it was all adrenaline. There were a lot of pounding walks to and from university with headphones blaring so loudly it worsened my tinnitus. When I moved to the Basque Country, I started listening to the things that made me feel again, music that caused an emotional response beyond loud and angry distraction.

I heard "Disorder" by mistake through the means of a generic 70s playlist and cried hysterical floods of tears. I listened to it over and over and over again, sobbing ridiculously and childishly in my new room, in my foreign apartment, with lots of floor space and zero relics of my DC-traumatised past. I was still so angry at him. DC had hurt me beyond all logical reason, but I could allow myself to feel an untampered, pure sorrow for Ian Curtis.

I listened to the song on repeat for weeks. The lyrics took on new meaning that I felt related entirely to me and DC. The sadness and emptiness he must have felt, our dependence on excessive drinking, the sex, the constant physical affection, the need for validation all summarised in one line, "Will these sensations help me feel the pleasures of a normal man?" Because we weren't normal. Both of us were desperately alone and in agonising pain and we hadn't really been aware of how heavily reliant we were on each other.

The floodgates opened. Suddenly, I started writing about him. I started crying for him because of the devastating sense of loss, as opposed to of out of anger from the injustice of it all. I wrote the delusional conversations. I scribbled shitty poems for him in class. I started to love him again and I listened to Joy Division. Then I found myself listening to New Order, especially their song "Ceremony."

Dan Collins' last completed piece was called "Ceremony." He gave it to a Mutual Friend of Great Importance who edited it as part of a university module. Our Mutual Friend of Great Importance edited it well. There was very little work to be done. The story was about a couple wandering through strange, Welsh lands with a baby that the narrator calls "the bundle" before being caught in this odd, witchlike cult. Towards the end there's an implication that the couple drown. It's very odd, very Wicker Man, very genius, deliberately overwritten and convoluted, as he himself acknowledged at the end of the story in the form of an editor's letter:

> *"As I've said, I won't trouble you for too long, good reader. But I think this note is necessary and may help you make sense of what is, I'm sure you'll agree, quite unnecessarily convoluted and oppressive language throughout the text."*

And what great writing, DC. You were always so, so good.

I once for in love with a lecturer who apologies for the words he chose *while* penning them down. I never related to anything more. DC uses a similar technique here. If you highlight your flaws, it helps to diminish them. People go, "Aha! At least they're self-aware!" At least, I hope that's what people say.

Ian Curtis' last song was also titled "Ceremony" and DC's last completed piece was called "Ceremony." The funeral was a ceremony, the song is about a funeral, the story is about a premature death, a funeral-like situation with bodies floating out to sea... there is something here that I agonised over like a mad detective. I may as well have been sticking pins in the story, connecting them to old Polaroids with lines of red thread for all it mattered. I never wished more than in these moments that Dan Collins' writing wasn't so completely facetious and opaque. Didn't he realise that I needed to establish meaning in all of this? Did Dan Collins know, as he was writing, that he was going to die?

But then there was another story. I don't think it was ever finished. "Horseshoe." It was supposed to be about witchcraft. He'd never tell anyone what was going to happen in his stories, even in workshops where it would have been incredibly helpful to know. Instead, he'd say: "Ah, you'll have to read it to find out," with a kind of wink whenever people asked where the piece was going. At one point I responded: "Yes, but for the sake of this workshop which you pay to attend, maybe it would be a good idea to let people know what it's about." At this point, I was tense. My patience was wearing thin, and I was getting pissed off with his pretentiousness, his belief that he was too good for the other writers around him. But everyone else found it very sweet and endearing, and they laughed at his mad, creative energy. I wanted to scream. He'd been cruel about my story "The Sudden Appearance of Bears" in the seminar, and I was resentful of how much everyone thought he was talented.

"Horseshoe" was an amazingly written story. It was a self-confessed rip-off of *Pale Fire* where DC had written a stunning villanelle, a style I attempted to emulate after his death in a poem titled "Dan Collins Could Have Written This Better." It's as self-indulgent and simplistic as the rest of my writing is. At least I know what I'm about, stylistically. DC's poem surrounded a demented mother taking medication in her wood hut with a beautiful sense of stylistic mysticism. Then he tore it apart line by line, analysing the relationship between the writer and his ex-wife until it became apparent something sinister was occurring. The mother/daughter relationship in the story was stiff and jilted, and there was a beautiful scene of her sucking on sweets, dejectedly. Here's the poem in its full:

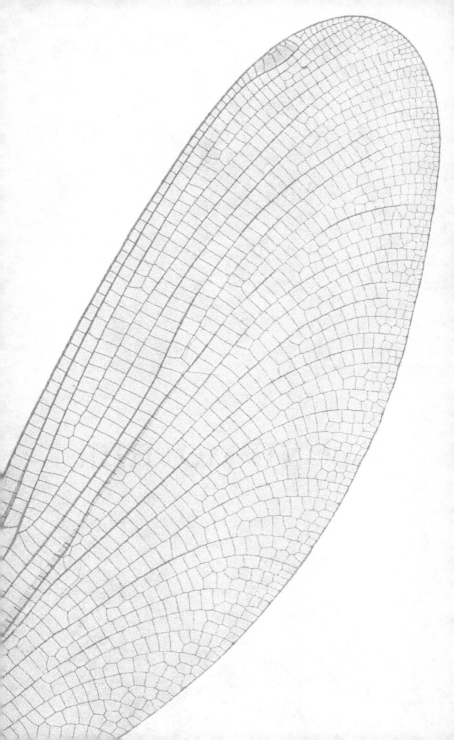

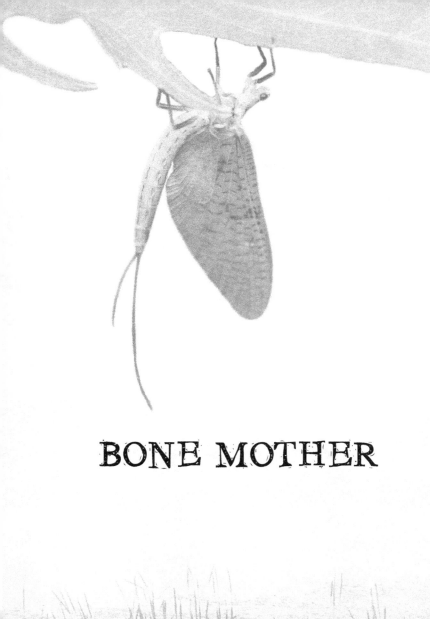

BONE MOTHER

Mother has donepezil in her mud hut,

In the hood of the forest she croaked,
Pushing her trolley through festering soot.

Reflected in the shop windows'
bright smut,
Her cracked hag's body is a sick joke,

Mother has donepezil in her mud hut.

When she fell, her head sparkled
with crimson,
Now a boy like a shell around a yolk,
Pushes her trolley through festering soot.

The trail leads from him to the
Mother's Cut,

Into a dream, under the Willow Oak,
Mother has donepezil in her mud hut.

On bonfire night, the cat got a haircut,
The boy sings his dead name, all-
the-way home,
Pushing her trolley through festering soot.

She must wait for the oven door to shut,

Now she opens windows, to clear
the smoke,

Mother has donepezil in her mud hut.

Pushing her trolley through festering soot.

It's a fucking good poem. It demonstrates
the extent of his talent, and the fact he goes on
to tear it apart through the voice of the narrator just adds a humbleness to the creativity
which I personally found charming. But what
would have happened at the end? He told me
his ideas about witchcraft, particularly about
the daughter of somebody who was alone and
dejected, who accused other women of witchcraft for her own amusement. Still, it was
only ever in the vague stages of development,
and he never liked to tell me too much until
it was totally perfect and completed, something I can't understand because I shove my
feelings and ideas at people so eagerly it's
embarrassing.

So, I pick apart his ideas and his words,
remembered and written, and I try to find purpose. It's become ceremonious in and of itself,
the reading of his notes, his writing, the unfin-
ished work "Horseshoe," the finished work
"Ceremony." Every time I look through it all,
I'm convinced that he must have been thinking
about death, even if not directly planning it. I
know he loved Joy Division because he was

angry about that one Wombat's song, and I think maybe he saw Ian Curtis as something to aim for. But then I read "Horseshoe" with its humour and its irony, and I think about how he wouldn't have been gathering ideas and planning to write them up if he knew he was going to die.

I'm taking down the photographs now. I'm pulling down the red lines of string. I'm putting away his words and his thoughts, and I'm attempting to embrace ignorance. I don't know why Dan Collins did what he did. I think it may have been out of spite, a punishment for me leaving him. I think he may have romanticised the early deaths of creative types and felt excited at the prospect of being a young tragedy. I think his relative's suicide attempt had a profound effect on him and perhaps he was copying her, maybe as a punishment too. I think he was in pain. I think he was psychotic and depressed. I think it was a moment of crisis where he may have acted without thinking. Sometimes I think he thought about it deeply. I think we'll never know. His words don't have answers, but they do have poetry, and doesn't that matter far more?

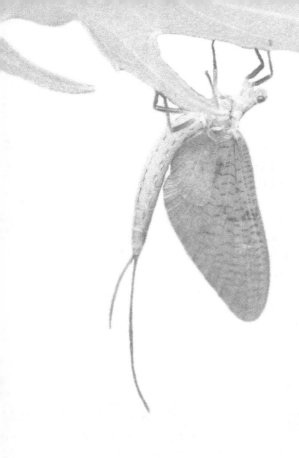

To the Girl

It's well overdue, but I think I owe a thank you to the girl with long black hair, twisted and clipped up in seminars, trailing down her back in dresses and up my nose when she lay next to me at night. I miss the awkward kisses, fingers trailing down bodies' sides, each thinking, "Is this okay? Am I doing alright?" I miss kissing her thighs. Thank you to the girl whose gasps still play in my head when I am lonely. Just gals being pals.

Except, I thank her partly because she *was* a pal, because she saw me cry and shake, with lumps in my throat, voice cracking and body in breakdown shivers. She saw the bitter hatefulness, the anger, and she stayed. She used her reassuring words to let me know it was okay. She kissed me, both of us with morning breath (we'd had maybe two hours of sleep) before we said goodbye at empty bus-stops. That night she'd let me sleep with my arm beneath her curving neck.

She called me on the anniversary of his death. She let me cry without reservation. She maybe didn't understand, but she tried. She knew there were feelings more important than jealousy. She listened. She empathised. She was reasonable. I think that this, more than anything, is love.

I thank the girl for showing me that intellect doesn't have to be cutting and cruel, that there can be talent without unjust superiority, that listening is valuable and kindness is free. I thank the girl for honesty, for building boundaries, for frank discussions about our feelings. I thank the girl for unceasing support, for love and loyalty, and for offering me beauty amongst so much pain.

Thank you to the girl whose kisses remind me that I am a human, the girl whose body dips inward for my arm's perfect placement, who speaks to me so gently that even in my worst state I know that I am safe.

I know she caught me at a terrible moment in my life. Had we addressed our stupid, little crushes before, then maybe things would have gone differently. Or maybe they wouldn't. It doesn't matter now.

Perhaps if the world was as kind and open-minded as she is, if there weren't so many oceans between us, we could still be together, forever wrapped up under bedsheets, tasting necklines, feeling pretty. Life doesn't work that way, but I can thank her.

So, to the girl,

Thank you. I love you. You're welcome back, any time.

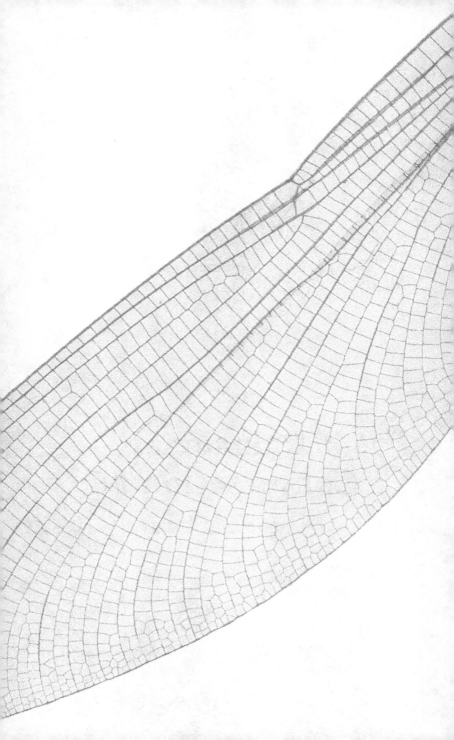

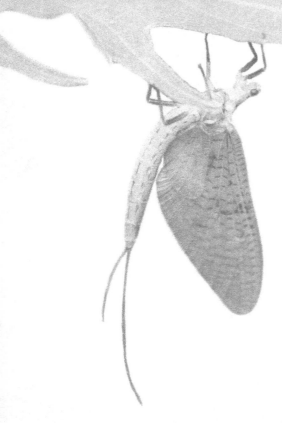

Delusional
Conversation #6:
A step backward

I'm back where I first began with these dangerous, helpless fantasies. I'm in the same coffee shop in the same port town in the Basque Country. I'm alone again. Again, this loneliness is not entirely my choice.

I'm struggling to build meaningful relationships here. I try to connect with people with brimming over-politeness, tumbling apologies, half-hearted conversations, but it only leads to humiliation. I miss you, DC. More accurately, I miss who I was when I was with you.

But perhaps that's also wrong. Wasn't I just as self-conscious, just as insecure, just as desperate for validation from those who didn't like me? It's hard to tell when we sugar-coat the past.

When I was last home, I told our Mutual Friends that I'd let the anger go. I wanted them to know that I was doing fine. The reality is though, I'm still angry and fearful and guilty. I don't know how to progress and stop myself from being this damaged mess.

DC, I've met someone I like to fuck who makes me feel nauseous. Every time I catch myself thinking about the way the Boy on the Beach looks, I feel these waves of sickness because I know I can't compare. He has beauty. He knows this. He plays with me. I know this. I'm complicit. I insult myself because I think that he might like it. I bring myself down to cater to his ego. I set myself up for the fall.

One of our treasured Mutual Friends asked me if I'm allowing myself to be used, putting myself on this destructive path towards inevitable heartbreak as a self-inflicted punishment for how I broke your heart. It's possible. However, I think it's more likely I'm doing this to prove a point: "I will get my heart broken and then I will not kill myself." If I handle pain and rejection from someone far less caring than I ever was to you, then I suppose that means you had no excuse. The suicide was not due to the intensity of your feelings towards me, it was entirely within your control, and I will know this when I am utterly estranged and lonely in a foreign country, heartbroken, with no one I can physically turn to. I'll want to die, but I'll choose not to. I will take the pain and accept my own responsibility for it.

But this is totally fucked up, and I know it. No counsellor will encourage me in this endeavour. No friend, no family member—no one is in favour of this plan. They look at me with confusion when I describe this new man, who I myself don't entirely like but who I am determined to let hurt me. Remember how strong you thought I was? How feminist and steadfast in my opinions? Not anymore, DC. I don't like myself that much anymore.

So, with this revealing background information regarding my current mental instability, I go back to watching the holograph of you, DC, sitting in front of me. I still hold onto a fondness for your sideburns, the cold expression behind your eyes, but your image is less clear to me this time around. You dress in waistcoats and velvet shirts. You are from another time, DC. It makes sense for me to think of you as living in the past because you do.

"DC, I'll ask you again. Did you ever love me?"

"I don't know," you say, although of course it's really me. "Do you love this new man?"

"No," I respond. "I'm not sure I even like him, but I feel horrified by the way he ignores me, and his transparent attempts to make me jealous, which of course all completely work. The thought of being rejected by him for someone prettier makes me feel sick."

"And are you acting in rational, logical ways that you understand?"

"Christ, no. I'm a nervous wreck actively observing myself sabotaging my own happiness while having no clue whatsoever how to stop it. What's worse is I know that I'm insufferable. I can understand completely why he'd stop wanting me."

"And would you do anything to keep him despite the fact it's making you miserable?"

"Yes."

"Why?"

"Because I've absurdly convinced myself that he's all I have right now, even though I know that isn't true."

"So, you have an unhealthy, illogical fixation with someone you're unsure if you even like, someone who makes you miserable and who you don't love, but you must keep him because your entire being feels like you depend on it?"

"Correct."

"So, ask me again."

"Did you ever love me, Dan Collins?"

"I don't know, Cathy. What do you think?"

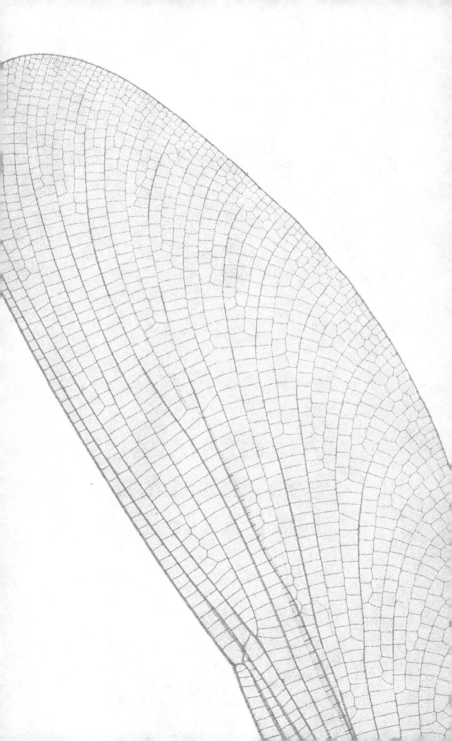

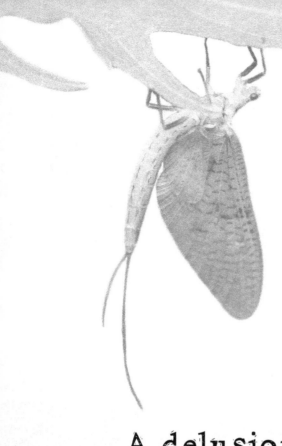

A delusional
conversation
with God

Today I went to church again, although to say "church" feels like an understatement. It was a beautiful cathedral in a small Spanish town. Real Spain, not the Basque Country. There was a museum and crypt attached to the church which attracted all faiths. European families ambled together alongside school trips with kids in squeaky shoes. People made "ooooo-hing" sounds at the sight of cherub sculptures and old scrolls. This is yet another place where people go to take photographs rather than pray. I can't say I mind. If anything, I find that more comforting and relatable. Perhaps I'm undeserving of self-reflection in a properly holy place. Praying was never a strong suit of mine.

I went with my family. They wanted to visit me in Spain but were unsure about the idea of the Basque Country what with the historical terrorism and general greyness surrounding the area. Santurtzi particularly is on the "wrong side" of the river, and it isn't all that entertaining for English people who could get a similar feeling in Bridlington or Hornsea. Instead, my family wanted to go somewhere more like a resort. There was a communal pool where we stayed and paella restaurants with a deliberately Mediterranean feel where no one minded the Spanglish that fell awkwardly from our mouths: *Dos cervezas, s'il vous plait, no por favor, no sorry...*

I flew out to meet them there. They're always welcome to come. I'd said that often enough, and I think they feel one port-town on the coast of Spain is very much the same as another. The place they chose was less overcast, and I was glad to escape from the lonely, summer monotony.

I separated from my parents when we reached the cathedral. This was okay. People didn't stick together here because it felt sacred, and sacredness is something best experienced alone. There was silence only interrupted by brief murmurs and coughs which, if anything, exemplified the quietness rather than spoiled it. Giant, mural-covered ceilings curved above me in blue and red. Figures joined together, making up the landscapes. Anguished faces peered down at me. Looking up, it felt like the sky was endless, even though we were all enclosed inside. There were sculptures like tombs lying in glass coffins. Jesus Christ spread out flat, the ribcage showing countable bones. Mary lay next to him, her dress as sky blue as the crayon I'm using to draft up this story (because we have a toddler with 500 spare toys, but not one adult, including the supposed writer, thought to bring a pen with them on holiday). I gazed at their calm, horizontal bodies. Crypts still feel strange.

I found an empty prayer room. High above the altar, there hung a life-sized, 3D sculpture of Jesus Christ on the cross. You could see the blood on his hands. There was silence now, completely. I walked down the aisle slowly, which I suppose was an attempt to show reverence. While I did this, I whispered internally. I apologised to Jesus and also to DC, for they both died for my sins.

I was alone, but there was no door to the room, just an alcove which people could walk past anytime, and this made me feel exposed. I stood underneath Jesus Christ and looked behind me as I dropped to my knees. These days dropping to my knees is always synonymous with blowjobs, and I felt angry at myself for thinking that in front of Jesus. I don't believe in God, but I do believe in good manners when it comes to the distinction between prayer and blowjob etiquette. Then again, examining the links between sexuality and Catholicism is so typical of Dan Collins that thinking about fellatio in that moment felt entirely appropriate.

I asked—if there was anyone there and if they were listening—that they were looking after Dan Collins. If it was Dan Collins listening, I asked for his forgiveness and hoped that he might look after me too, perhaps with some of the supernatural abilities proffered to the deceased. I'm not a spiritual person as I continue to say, but I hate to think of him in that hole in the ground, rotting. I'd like to think that his brain could still exist to think up sardonic jokes. If there was anything omniscient listening, which I doubted, I wanted them to know that I was thinking of him and wishing him well, to let him know I'd forgiven him, and that I hoped he'd forgiven me too, for what I'm not entirely sure, but I still felt the need for vindication from somewhere. There was more, but I can't remember the panicked thoughts that ran through my head. I just know that afterward, I felt something like "at peace."

I would have liked to sit for a while, but instead I stood again and stared at Jesus. My phone buzzed, a text from the Boy on the Beach who I desperately needed to adore me. He asked me if I was free, if I wanted to join him in bed for a little fun. It was all in jest. He knew I was away and was presumably hoping for written encouragement, an idea that he could use to help himself (I am surprisingly meek with this kind of thing, which means the two creative writing degrees I agonised over are utterly useless for anything practical whatsoever). I wasn't in the mood, so I sent a picture of Jesus' agonised face and asked him if he felt guilty for his heathenism. I thought it was funny. Dan Collins would have found it funny. The Boy on the Beach did not. I could tell he was irritated I'd ruined the mood from his half-hearted and humourless response, so I threw him a bone and asked him if he would like a blowjob on a religious altar instead. The sin is what made it so tempting, and anyway I'm often inspired by my current surroundings.

"Not really, to be honest," he responded.

"Oh, no?" I asked, feeling as embarrassed as I'm sure he intended me to feel.

"Yeah, call me weird. I just never found religion sexy."

I wanted to explain to him the salaciousness of confession booths, the universality of the "sexy nun" costume, the way that celibacy makes way for deep sexual tension, and tension is really where true, authentic sexuality lies. As soon as that tension is released, there are just sweaty limbs and a vague sense of comfortable disorientation, but before the shudder, there is power at its peak. I wanted to say that I thought dropping to your knees was something submissive and beautiful and holy but also synonymous with blowjobs. Instead, I let the conversation die.

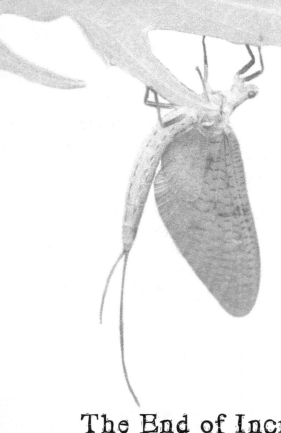

The End of Incredibly
Short-Lived,
Disappointing New Love

Being a martyr is dull. I was determined, so, so determined, to be heartbroken and rejected. Then I could rise from the ashes strong, a phoenix despite my battle scars. I waited fearfully for the confirmation that I was worthless, that I was nothing worth dying over, just an ordinary girl who will have her self-worth accurately put in place by superior people.

Don't worry, I'm sure that's all going to come in time. I've been rejected before. I've had my heart broken. I've been a trainwreck in the mess that is unrequited love. Who hasn't? But with the Boy on the Beach, this wasn't one of those situations.

The actual argument which caused the breakup is insignificant. Plans to meet up got messy and convoluted. When I arrived, he was distant and flirtatious with others. I felt unwelcome, I was called clingy, so I chose to act cold, et cetera, et cetera. His passive aggression turned to outright aggression. I suggested that the argument may have been fabricated by Boy on the Beach because he wasn't interested in me anymore, and perhaps that was true, although perhaps I'm needlessly paranoid. He became incensed, in the way that only men who are accused of doing something they've done become incensed. I was insane, "nuts," paranoid. There was something deeply wrong with me, he claimed. I asked, "Is this not gaslighting?" The suggestion was regarded as even more insane.

The argument is petty and universal I imagine, the same kind of thing that occurs in all couples and isn't abusive or evil or noteworthy, but simply mean. These occurrences demonstrate that people aren't as compatible as they originally thought. The difference is that I believed him. I cried and apologised and admitted that I was insane, but only because of my trauma, only because I was so, terribly damaged by my last boyfriend, (who killed himself, don't you know?) and I was working so hard to be better. This was accepted. We were okay.

Except that I felt terrible afterward because despite how much I try to diminish my self-worth, there's still this nagging voice in the back of my head. I picture her as me when I was sixteen or seventeen, insecure and unreliable, but still forthright in her feminist views, still wearing Bikini Kill t-shirts and too much eyeliner, questioning her sexuality, alongside the point of all men. She's still gonna be there waving around Sylvia Plath poetry and reminding me to get a fucking grip. It doesn't matter how much I love someone or how much I hate myself, that voice is going to be there, whiny and self-indulgent, but surprisingly correct more often than not. I like to picture this person as my own Jiminy Cricket except more aggressive and likely to derail conversations in A-Level English classrooms. I listened to her. I left. I never thought that I could leave another relationship again after how badly it had ended before, especially someone I'd been so smitten with, but I did it. Madness. I must still like myself a little bit.

I've learned that self-esteem isn't something you either have or don't have. It requires constant work and evaluation. Passive insecurity and self-loathing is actually much, much easier. I think the trick, at least for me, is to pretend that you're somebody else, somebody you already deem worthy of respect. Eventually, it becomes natural. Now, I'm not one for the RuPaul/Queer Eye, "slay, honey," "queen, work," "if you can't love yourself…" mythology. I'm cynical about standing in front of mirrors and repeating that "I AM FIERCE, HUNTY" because that will never be who I am. Not everyone is beautiful, clever, and exceptional. I won't pretend I'm all those things in the hopes I can force others to see that too. Perhaps though, I can accept that I have to put boundaries in place for my own personal happiness, and that those who cross those boundaries have to go, not out of any empowered, feminist choice, but just because they have to. If someone cheats on you, abuses you, hits you, or even if they're just a little bit of a prick and they make you feel unworthy of them, it's best to shrug your shoulders and go: "Well, if this is their behaviour, I have to remove myself from the situation. It's a shame, but it's out of my control."

I don't think people should do this because they're too beautiful, funny, clever, exciting, interesting, sexy, and driven. I also don't think people should leave because of imaginary better options waiting in the side-lines. I think people should do it because they're people. Full stop. People deserve to be treated well.

I said before that I would never be with anyone I wasn't devoted to entirely, that I'd have to be willing to put up with the absolute worst behaviour rather than leave because I could never accept the risk of breaking someone's heart again. I don't think that anymore. I'm sure that Boy on the Beach isn't heartbroken. He'll recover, and judging by his popularity, I imagine quite quickly too. It might be disappointing for him, but it's for the best. He knows this.

Boy on the Beach is not an evil abuser, or at least, he wasn't to me. I've portrayed him unfairly in my insecurity as some kind of revenge for my unwelcome feelings of affection. He was a nice lad, although a little cocky, who didn't care for me as deeply as I cared for him. I don't want to be waiting around for texts that tell me when to set off, or cancelled on at the last minute, or told to wait around in a city centre for hours before I can come round. It's annoying. But it isn't evil. I was wrong for him because in my trauma-induced state, I need reassurance that people aren't angry at me all the time. That can be trying.

If the world is kind, he'll find someone with less trauma, I'll find someone with more compassion, and we'll both be alright. Maybe my ending this relationship is a sign my self-esteem is back. I may be turning into the pre-DC Cathy I never appreciated before. Perhaps it's a sign that I'm destroying the things that make me happy. Time will tell, I suppose. Still, post-breakup, I have this feeling in my gut like anxious euphoria, like I've dropped MD but I don't need to worry about the jaw-ache. I'm sure I'll be shaken and hurt if I see him around with someone new, but I'll recover. I mean, fuck me, I've recovered from worse.

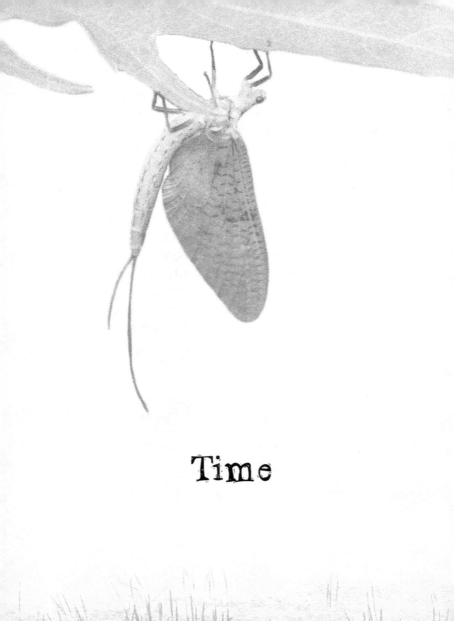

Time

See, I don't know if I'm experiencing time correctly. I no longer have time for the important things like reading, laundry, cherishing my loved ones, writing thank you cards, or fucking strangers to get that super squeaky thrill of being alive. I want to have a nine-and-a-half-hour sleep, but there's no time because there's always work, you know, and weekend plans, like now we're heading to Galicia on a fourteen-hour car trip, just to "chew the hay and shoot the shit," (needless to say I'm going with Americans) and this will likely change my life! Or something. See, I do this shit a lot, and it's always life-affirming in a kind of way. I mean the kind of way in that while I'm doing it, I'm thinking, "Wow, I bet in the future I'll remember this as life-affirming; this could be a happy memory someday, if I ever got my shit together and stopped thinking about some hypothetical, near-distant future," you know, that kind of way. I spend a lot of time traipsing up mountains, seeing beaches with white sand, examining architecture I know nothing about, all the while thinking, "Yeah, this is alright," like, "Look how well I'm doing on my fourteen-hour car trip, seeing Europe from a car seat, taking exhausted breaths in port towns where it smells like sea-salt and fish," which is always regarded as unpleasant, but I don't think it is. The only thing unpleasant is the thought of a hook through a lip, a flopping body smacked, shocked dead, but I'm not a vegetarian, so I don't think about that shit, especially not in port towns while I'm breathing in the fresh air and savouring the time I should be using to become a linguist, but I won't learn this language because I'm not likely to stay. Life's too short and I've too little time left to give away.

All these weekend trips look nice in pictures while I show everyone how much of a good time I'm having with all the time I have to spend because time is fleeting and it never lasts forever, don't you know? And obviously, I don't just mean time, I mean youth, which is already slipping. I have wrinkles on my forehead now and stains on my teeth. I could pass for around forty (and yet somehow I still have acne? Which I pick at constantly, despite the scars and scabs and dents it leaves). I should be trying harder not to smoke or drink black tea. I should consume my meals in the style of liquid green. I should drink teas with honey, and moisturise my skin, but why can't I enjoy myself for now? I'm young and youth is fleeting, god it is. I think I'll light this cigarette and think about dead fish.

But, man, when am I gonna find the time to do my laundry? When will I plan that novel, or that fucking PhD? The only time I ever truly feel alive is in the walls inside a university. So, I'm keeping on, keeping on, keeping on planning on writing, but it's just so hard to find the time, you know? With work and sleep and anxious panting, and I'm writing right now, but I'm thinking, "Please, be sensible, this shit's a pipe dream, and you need a full eight hours of sleep because insomnia's been keeping you awake as of late, even when you're knackered from the work, the trips, the gym, so now's the time to wind it down and get to bed," but I don't have the time to do that, so I'll sleep when I'm dead, and I wish that when I said that I felt rock-and-roll, but instead I just feel stressed, but it's alright because it's good to be busy. When you're busy, you don't think, so you're distracted from the misery, except Christ, you know, not really, because it still comes in pangs that leave me doubled over, and I still pound the concrete when I'm walking with my headphones in blaring too loudly while I worry about tinnitus. These days, my rucksack is always disjointingly heavy from the gym (you know, with water bottles, towel, clothes, the lot) and all the books and extra things I have every intention of squeezing in in that spare hour between lunch and getting thin, but fuck they're getting coffee now, and I need to go too because I need to FIT IN, but I never fit in the time for everything, and I realise that routine is so demoralising. I must schedule more time for spontaneity.

This is why I like to meditate, so I'm meditating now and thinking, "This is good." I carved out a nice little spot for self-care, but this whole time I'm aware that I don't really need ten minutes to sit and breathe when there's laundry to do, cats in England to feed (dying cats, no less, I mean aged sixteen, it's any day now, and I'm wasting time being here, far away and experiencing my life to the fullest, when I could be with my cat sleeping wrapped up in blankets on the absolute dullest, Yorkshire, autumn day), but this is bad because I'm thinking when I need to clear my mind. You call it "noting" when you realise you're thinking, so dismiss the thought and go back to your breathing.

I have noted I am thinking about my dying cat.

In... out... in... out...

I scan down my body to feel for sensations, and I realise that one side of my face is drooping, and I wonder how common it is to have a stroke without noticing, and it's probably not a stroke. I need to keep tabs on my hypochondria, you know? Actually, it feels like a cluster of spots on one side of my cheek, (or maybe larger than a spot, maybe a bite, although it's too late for mosquitos so I assume I've been bitten by ants, and they'll lay their eggs under my skin, and the flesh will burst open when they're fully grown, and the ants will crawl over my face and into my ears and my eyeballs and devour me from the inside out)—

NOTING NOTING NOTING.

In, out, in, out.

I really need to sleep, but instead I check my cheek to be sure that underneath the skin there's nothing in there moving, and instead I see that every inch of me is covered with fine, blonde hair. I don't know if that's normal or if I'm some kind of hormonally imbalanced freak, and I should go to the doctor but I don't have any time between my work and gym and sleep and weekend trips and laundry, and writing down my pipe dreams, and PhD proposals, and being busy, not unhappy, no, just busy being busy, being busy, being.

And I wonder when I'm going to find the time to get over you. They say that it takes time. I don't have any more time left to be taken. I don't have time to analyse, I don't have time to move on, and I don't know how I had the time to fall in love to begin with. Somehow, in the past, I always found the time for you.

But now, I don't have time to pine over photographs, I don't have time to dwell and cry, I don't have time to regret, but somehow it still sneaks in, tears crawling in with sweat when I'm running at the gym, and I'm pounding on the treadmill, and I'm still not fitting it, and I think about all the ways I don't measure up because of battered face and hip fat, sure, but also because there's something intrinsically, sincerely incorrect about me, some flaw in my brain that makes being around others a chore because it doesn't matter where I happen to be, there will always be this unnamed thing that's wrong within me, and I don't mean this to make me sound interesting or damaged because Christ knows that kind of bullshit is something I can't stand.

And I think about how you hurt me, and I know that now you're fine. I know that, with time, I too will be just fine because I hate myself just slightly less than I drastically loved you. I think about all the things I need to change about myself, all the situations in which I could now place myself and the thing is, despite it all, if I gave in and let myself fail, and drank myself into a stupor... If I moved to a squat and took up performance art or punk guitar with every intention of dying at twenty-seven from an accidental overdose in an effortlessly cool, broken glass-like setting... If I stopped everything and moved to the other side of the planet, and drank fresh kale, and I did yoga on the beach and learned to breathe effortlessly with the sea... If I read self-help books, and acted with love, and dedicated my time to building wells in Kenya, volunteering in refugee camps in Uganda, spreading the power of love and positivity, if I gave away my possessions to help the poor and needy, dedicating myself entirely to selflessness... If I cut my wrists with a burned out razor blade, and lay curled up in a dirty bathtub waiting for the door to knock, if I left posters inside the apartment block to let everyone know that this wasn't anybody's fault, if I took so many pills I couldn't feel myself throw up the organs that I needed to keep breathing, and I finally knew what it was like not to overthink, none of it would help.

And I don't have the time to keep on trying one more time. I can't just keep rebooting. These fresh starts are a lie. There is no place to be safe when your heart is breaking for yourself, and while I don't know what I want, I know just what I could use right now.

What a privilege it's been to find the time for a nervous breakdown.

Important Clarity

Reader, I fucked up. In the last chapter, I indicated that I ended my relationship with dignity. This is a lie. I went back to the Boy on the Beach multiple times. I lay on my side in his sad double bed, staring at his back after a meaningless fuck I was already starting to regret. I let my feelings develop stronger, against my better judgement, and found a reason to justify all of it. I sabotaged things for myself with my insecurity. I put up with what I knew was gaslighting because I was so scared of being alone. I was weak. This led to a very public drunken breakdown where I begged him to want me, and he didn't.

I suppose that things worked exactly as I intended them to. I found someone I cared enough about to know that I would never have the strength to leave them. I punished myself very efficiently. I got my heart broken, away from home, and I do want to kill myself, but I won't. I wish I could end this book on a high-note and say that everything was okay, but it wasn't really, in the end.

Even in bad times, I'm trying to force myself to remember that there's always coffee, there's always cigarettes, there's always beer and concerts and new books coming out and there's so much left to read and music left to listen to and bullshit left to write. A broken heart won't stop this. Self-loathing and humiliation may in fact encourage this. I'm often a lot more productive when I'm feeling self-absorbed, and who is more self-absorbed than the heartbroken? The world will keep spinning and there are things more important than a Boy on a Beach with a shitty hand tattoo.

I wish Dan Collins would've had this realisation. I wish he'd sat in a bar in a port-town in Spain and drank a glass of wine and cried. I wish he'd shivered in the rain and let the shame buckle him. I wish he'd listened to Joy Division and masturbated in the shower and thought about all the good sex he wouldn't get to have anymore. I wish he'd taken a deep breath and let the self-hatred, loss, and pain flush through him and realised that there are things in life more important than some girl in a lecture hall with a shitty thigh tattoo and a mediocre writing style.

But he is not me and I am not him, and I feel what I feel, which maybe isn't what he felt. I know I'm not stable. Neither was he. But we are different, and this punishment might have been unnecessary. In fact, I know it was and I knew it even at the time. I did this self-destructive thing because I didn't like myself and this is all part of the low self-esteem that comes from a lifetime of bullshit like this. I'm going to get better though. I don't know if I'll ever be exactly the same, but I'm going to keep trying to move forward, to be less self-deprecating, less melodramatic, to be more myself and to care less what other people think of that. A positive attitude doesn't always help, and anyway I suppose I don't have to be happy all the time. Maybe I won't be happy. Maybe I'm not a happy person. But I will be alive. That's something.

When I left the Basque Country, for good this time, my friends got me a framed picture. It was a collection of photographs with all of us together, and a sweet message reminding me I was always part of the cuadrilla. It was very sweet, and I was touched.

The frame, of course, smashed in my suitcase. There are now slithers of glass glittering inside one if its zipped up pockets. I gingerly recovered the picture with my fingers, trying to pick off the pieces still stuck there but, unfortunately, they were glued on. It's fine if I keep it on a high shelf away from face-rubbing, geriatric cats and baby nephews. I have to remember though, that I can't touch it. These memories are covered in broken glass.

White Butterflies

He wasn't the first man I'd ever loved, but he was the first man I'd ever loved who then went on to kill himself, and I suppose that gives him a particular significance in the grand scheme of my life. I remember sitting outside with his mother while she handed over all the things from his will. This was during the part of the grieving process where I drank myself to near-death just trying to get through the weeks. A white butterfly landed on the wooden table of that bright British beer-garden, and his mother told me, her eyes wet and shining like goldfish, that whenever she saw a white butterfly, she liked to think it was her son saying hello, promising he was still watching over her. I've never been able to prevent cynicism from twisting my crooked, facial features. For this, naturally, I detest myself.

In an attempt to improve my future prospects, and also to ease my way into an early cirrhosis of the liver, I moved to mainland Europe where the wine is cheaper and there were fewer people there who loved me enough to worry about that fact. Through sheer will-power and psychological repression, I forgot everything about my life from *before* and assumed that this, right now, was *it*. There was no past. There was no dead lover, no abandoned tombstone, and if I couldn't gain approval from these new, fashionable Europeans, and if I couldn't force this updated, troubled boy to shower me with adoration, then life was worthless. My failure would confirm that I was entirely unlovable and destined to die alone. So, I cried and pined pathetically, giving my heart to anyone who was cold and attractive enough that I thought they might be able to fix it, as though to fix a broken heart you require broad shoulders and good cheekbones. I thought that by seeking approval and caring too much I was demonstrating that I was a good, empathetic person, but I've since learned compassion isn't really compassion if you only ever direct it towards the people you want to fuck.

At home, a sea away, a two-hour flight and a three-hour train, a friend of mine was suffering. This wasn't a friend I'd ever tried to impress. He knew me back when I had braces and poorly dyed hair, when we made cringey YouTube videos and spent too long putting on Halloween make-up, singing along to Paramore, both deluded in thinking that the future would be better for us. We hadn't spoken for a while. The last time was the day before my flight when he asked me to keep in touch, and I said I would and then I didn't.

Away from him, in this new country, I cut off bits of myself to fit into a mould of a clique that didn't suit me. I tried to manipulate people who couldn't understand me into loving me, so desperate for a fresh start that I didn't consider all the loose ends I'd left behind. I don't know what my friend was doing during all this time. Perhaps it was something similar. All I know is that he must have been suffering to do what he did.

And he wasn't the first man I'd ever loved, or indeed the first man I'd ever loved who then went on to kill himself, but—as I wish I could tell any teenager, crying naked and lonely between soiled bedsheets—your firsts aren't always as significant as you think.

After my friend's funeral, I lay in my back garden, allowing my black dress to soak in the heat, feeling the sweat gathering underneath my breasts and chafing where my armpits met the cloth. It's impossible to sleep the night before a funeral. I was so exhausted, reality was made fuzzy. I rolled over onto my stomach, resting my head on top of my hands, allowing the sun to burn my legs as much as it desired. Before I slept, I kept my eyes open just long enough to see two white butterflies fluttering around the green and purple flowers, dancing with each other like ghosts, and I wished that I could take a picture before I stopped and wondered, who the hell for? They kissed the petals and so I closed my eyes. I slept long enough to learn that a gentle breeze through summer trees is the most sympathetic alarm clock known to man. The butterflies were gone, but I remembered them and smiled.

I asked myself, if I was really so cynical then why did this image bring me so

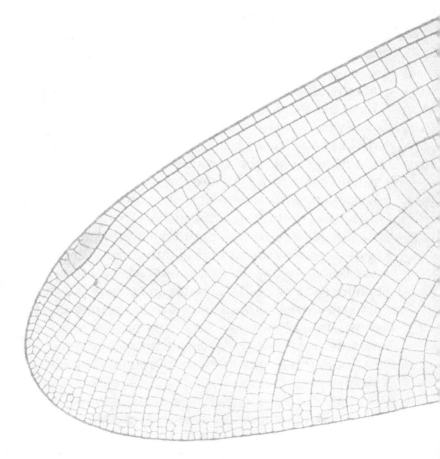

much comfort? Why did a passing remark made two years before and heard through a haze of drunkenness stick with me when I clearly neglect to remember so much that's important? Strange, I thought. So strange.

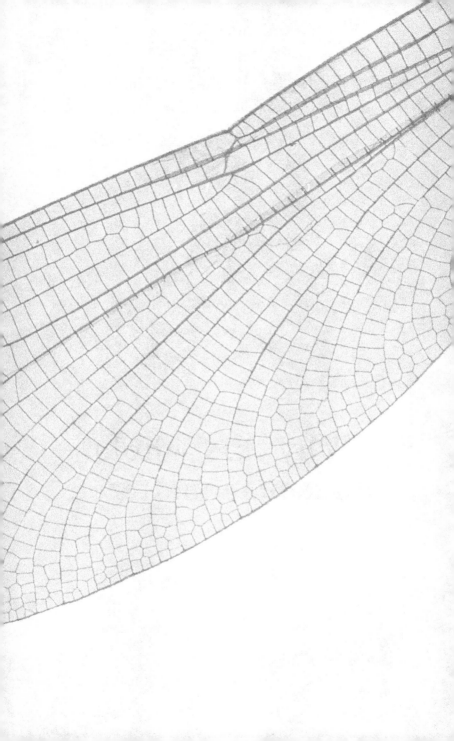

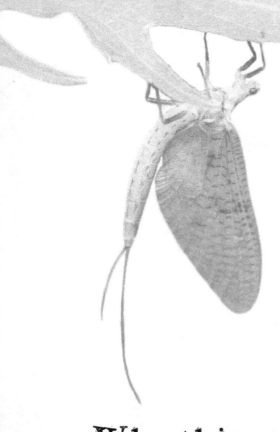

Why this whole
nonsense mattered

Sometimes, when I'm working on creative projects which require research, where I need to change my voice to fit into a character or where the plot is something I have to plan instead of something I get to live, I find things a bit overwhelming. Then I think about DC and all the things I want to say, and I wonder if writing is better when it isn't forced. Already, pen to paper, things are rolling quite smoothly. Like stretching, I feel some kind of loosening, some release. The air enters my lungs a little easier. The knot in my stomach is forgotten. Now look, I have a paragraph. I can feel proud.

It's really about quality, not quantity. An outstanding haiku is better than a mediocre trilogy. I'm not sure the quality of this work is particularly high, but the fact that I shovelled out 30,000 words of sheer self-pity in six months should be testament to something. This was therapy. I'd like to think I'm in some way heading towards being healed. Maybe for that purpose, quantity can be better than quality. For therapeutic purposes, I'd rather have three bottles of cheap vodka than one glass of expensive champagne.

I always struggled to keep diaries. I have a million old notebooks starting on January 1st, and nearly all of them were neglected by the 10th. I remember once, as a kid, I filled a notebook with an entry every single day until the whole book was full, and then immediately threw it in the outside bin. That seemed very important to me at the time. I don't wish I had that notebook back either. The things I wrote in it as a child were troubled and unkind.

And Marvel is a diary full of troubled and unkind things. I suppose that's all it's ever really been. Its function is to track and secure my thoughts so I can get some sense of validation. In words, we have a clearer narrative.

I'm not arrogant enough to presume I could write self-help. While this writing may have been my therapy, I do very much need actual therapy. But I do want to put this somewhere. I think it might be helpful to some other insecure wreck of a girl going through something similar. I think that I, eighteen months ago, could have done with a book telling me I wasn't completely alone.

Death is hard. Suffering doesn't make you stronger. But it's as inevitable as manipulation and misogyny, as love, conflict, insanity, sleep-deprivation, and broken hearts. It's coming. It's here. This is how I coped. I hope you enjoyed the show.

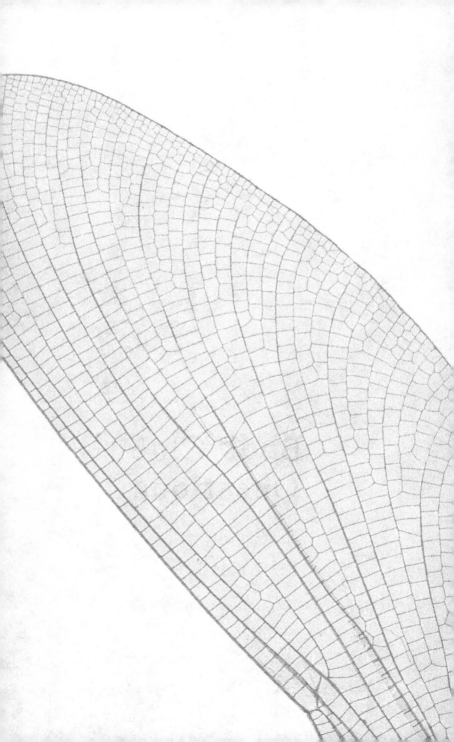

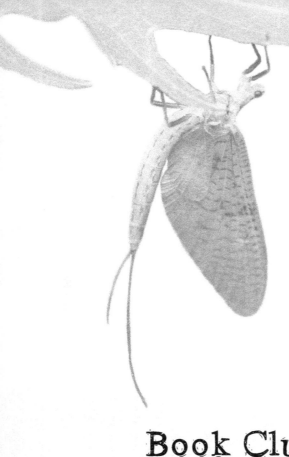

Book Club
Questions

1) Who are confessional memoirs written for: the audience or the writer?

2) Do you ever keep a journal for therapeutic reasons? If so, do you find it useful?

3) Why do you think society quickly looks for people to blame when faced with suicide?

4) Why do you believe so many young men are dying from suicide in recent years? Is it toxic masculinity or a lack of mental health resources? Is this a problem you yourself have noticed?

5) Why do you think there was so much use of religious iconography in memories of Dan Collins?

6) Are personal memoirs about dead people ethical or exploitative?

7) This journal, including the poetry, was left largely unedited. Why do you think this was?

8) Is the authenticity worth the messiness of prose?

9) What effect does entitlement and flawed romantic representations have on the psyches of young people muddling their way through relationships?

10) Everyone here is kept nameless, except for DC and the writer herself. Why do you think that is?

11) Who owns the rights to dead people's poetry? Their suicide notes?

12) Was it worth writing this book?

13) What do you take away?

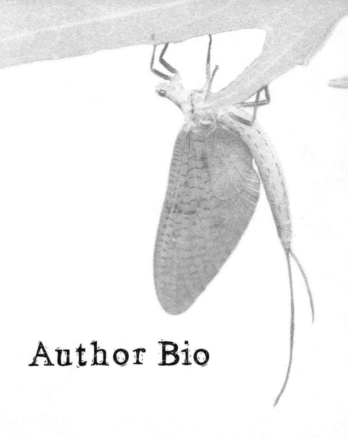

Author Bio

Cathleen Davies is a writer from East Yorkshire. Their work has appeared in various magazines and anthologies. Their debut collection of short-stories *Cheeky, Bloody Articles* was published by 4Horsemen in 2022. This is their second solo publication.

More books from
4 Horsemen Publications

Literary & Short Story Collections

Cathleen Davies
Cheeky, Bloody Articles

Anthologies & Collections

4HP Anthologies
Teen Angst: Mix Vol. 1
Teen Angst: Mix Vol. 2
My Wedding Date
The Offices of
Supernatural Being
The Sentient Space

Demonic Anthologies
Demonic Wildlife
Demonic Household

Demonic Carnival
Demonic Classics
Demonic Vacations
Demonic Medicine
Demonic Workplace
& more to follow!

XXX- Holiday Collection
Unwrap Me
Stuffing My Stocking

Coloring Books

Jenn Kotick
Mermaids

Discover more at
4HorsemenPublications.com